The Last Full Measure

The Last Full Measure

Ann Rinaldi

Harcourt

Houghton Mifflin Harcourt

Boston   New York   2010

Harcourt is an imprint of the Houghton Mifflin Harcourt Publishing Company.

www.hmhbooks.com

Text set in Adobe Garamond

Library of Congress Cataloging-in-Publication Data
Rinaldi, Ann.
The last full measure / Ann Rinaldi.
p. cm.
Summary: In 1863 Pennsylvania, fourteen-year-old Tacy faces the horrors of the Battle of Gettysburg while trying to stay out of the way of her brother David, who is in charge while their father serves as a doctor in the Union army, and to keep her friend Marvelous, a free black, safe from rebel soldiers.
Includes bibliographical references.
ISBN 978-0-547-38980-6 (hardcover : alk. paper) 1. Gettysburg, Battle of, Gettysburg, Pa., 1863—Juvenile fiction. 2. United States—History—Civil War, 1861-1865—Juvenile fiction. [1. Gettysburg, Battle of, Gettysburg, Pa., 1863—Fiction. 2. United States—History—Civil War, 1861-1865—Fiction. 3. Family life—Pennsylvania—Fiction. 4. Brothers and sisters—Fiction. 5. African Americans—Fiction. 6. Pennsylvania—History—Civil War, 1861-1865—Fiction.] I. Title.
PZ7.R459Lar 2010
[Fic]—dc22
2009049980

Manufactured in the United States of America
DOC 10 9 8 7 6 5 4 3 2 1

4500261631

For Gil Spencer,

a newspaper person's newspaper editor who taught me much about writing

CHAPTER ONE

Gettysburg, Pennsylvania
June–July, 1863

"WHERE ARE YOU GOING, TACY?"

Sam was on me again. He was always on me, spying, watching my every move, hoping to catch me at some misadventure so he could report it to my mother or my brother David and make winning points for himself.

I was in trouble all the time on account of Sam Wade, the twelve-year-old hired boy. Even though Jennie Wade, his older sister, was my friend.

I was halfway out the back door when he caught me, near out into the sweet June evening, the fireflies beckoning me invitingly.

There was nothing for it. I had to tell him. "Marvelous hasn't come home again. Her daddy was around, asking if I could fetch her. She only comes if I fetch her."

"Damned darkie—why do you care?"

"She's my friend."

"Friend?" He made a scoffing sound. "How many times already have the lot of them made riots by rushing through town at the slightest rumor of the Rebs coming, tearing and wrecking as they go?"

"They're scared is all, Sam. Wouldn't you be if you

were black and the Rebs were coming? They're scared of being sold into slavery."

"They're free, ain't they? All hundreds of them we gots here."

"They won't be when the Rebs arrive. Now get out of my way. I've got to fetch Marvelous home before dark comes down."

He grinned. His freckled face, the blond hair falling over it, the confident attitude, plagued me. He liked to act as if he had more assurance than I did in my own house. "I'm gonna tell your brother."

"Go ahead. I don't care." I broke past him and ran down the back path, through the horse pasture, and toward the woods. I knew the way to the hiding place the darkies had outside of town, where they took refuge when they thought the Rebels were coming.

And they *were* coming. Telegrams said that they had already taken Fairfield, eight miles away. Many citizens had closed up their houses and left on the trains. Merchants had hidden most of their goods because they heard the Rebs were coming. Governor Andrew Curtin had issued orders this month for fifty thousand additional troops for the Pennsylvania Militia.

And the last time Pa was home, after doing his doctoring at Antietam and all those other battles in the South, he and David had had *the argument.*

With David shouting yes, he *was* going to enlist in the militia. And Pa saying no he was not! Not with that twisted leg of his, he was not! He was staying right here at home and taking care of the place and his mother and sister!

And then Pa adding, "Go, if you want, go and try to enlist. Don't listen to me. See if they take you."

After Pa left, David did go to enlist. And they turned him down. So he lost his final chance to become a Union soldier like my other brothers, Brandon and Joel, who are both officers with the Second Pennsylvania Cavalry.

That last fight between David and Pa embittered David even more than he'd been up until now, so that, though he'd been slowly turning away from me since the war started and Pa wouldn't let him go for a soldier, in the last few weeks he scarce spoke to me at all. Oh, he still spoke to Ma. He was still respectful and kindly to her, but mostly he kept to himself, staring off into some middle distance, smoking his cheroots, or reading or strumming his banjo.

He no longer talked with me about my books or schoolwork from the Young Ladies' Seminary, although school was out now. He no longer read poetry to me. Whatever we had between us was broken, strewn into bits and pieces on the ground between us, like broken glass, keeping us from getting any closer to each other, from reaching out and remembering what we once had. And we had a lot, though I am only fourteen and he is twenty-one.

He growls at me now. He orders me around. "If I'm to take care of you as Pa wants, I'll take care of you," he says.

It's a threat, not a promise. I stay out of his way.

There are different ways the war can take a brother from you.

When Ma receives letters from Brandon or Joel and reads them aloud, David excuses himself and leaves the room.

And I've had to go to Ma. For David's sake, not for mine. To Ma, who still believes in everything: that the sun will rise every morning, that God has His eye on the sparrow, that her boys will be protected in the war, and that General Robert E. Lee, when he comes, won't really do us any harm. Because, after all, he's a Southern gentleman, isn't he?

Ma and Pa both come from Virginia.

"Ma, David's been imbibing rum in the barn at night."

"He'll be all right, darling. David's a good boy."

"Lots of rum, Ma. Sometimes he's really in his cups."

"David can hold his liquor, like all gentlemen can," Ma said. "He's just trying to hide his sorrow at not being able to go to war."

David didn't always have his twisted leg. He got it when he was about fourteen, when he was out riding and his horse tripped and fell on him. Pa operated on him and tried to right the leg, but too many bones were crushed. Pa sent him to Philadelphia to important doctors there. They could do nothing, either.

Ma still insists the leg "will be right again someday." Ma refuses to see what she doesn't want to see. It's a gift. I wish I had it.

It took me about twenty minutes to get to the dar-kies' hiding place. I'd been there before. Marvelous had shown it to me. The darkies, and we had at least four hundred of them in Gettysburg, lived southwest of town. They worked on farms, or for families. Basil Biggs, daddy of Marvelous, had a two-horse team and worked on a farm. His wife, Mary, did our laundry. There was also a shopkeeper and a shoemaker, and many were laborers in town.

The hideaway they had chosen was in a thicket of woods north of us. Here they had tents set up, caves dug in the hills, fireplaces made of stone, provisions hidden, wood stacked, everything needed to live in the open for days, even weeks. It was deserted now, of course, because no Rebs were here yet.

I wandered about, calling her name. "Marvelous, it's me, Tacy. You must come out now. It's getting dark. Your daddy wants you home. He's powerful worried about you."

She came in her own good time, a small quiet creature holding her own lantern, whispering my name, saying how glad she was to see me.

She was a beautiful girl, compact, neat in her person, her dark curly hair in tow with a ribbon, her round face bright with hope, her eyes sparkling.

We hugged. "Oh, Tacy, how good of you to care about me. Do you think we can get home before dark?"

The dusk was giving way to darkness. The last vestiges of sun were a sloppy streak across the western sky. The angels would soon wipe it away. "Come, we must be quick about it," I said.

But when we turned around the path blended in with the landscape. There seemed, as a matter of fact, to be two paths and too many bushes all over the place. And then there were voices where there should not be voices.

Of a sudden, out of the bushes and shadows, two figures loomed.

"So, there you are, you disobedient little wretch. Out of the house without permission. What did I tell you about that, eh? What did I tell you I'd do next time you did that?"

God in heaven, my brother David! And, grinning behind him, holding a lantern, Sam.

Then my arm was pulled, unceremoniously, by David, and the next thing I knew he had hauled me across his middle and was whacking me on my bottom, one, two, three, four, five, with a hard, unforgiving hand, and a harder, unforgiving heart. I could not free myself from his grasp. He'd never hit me before. No one had. And I knew somehow that the strokes were not for me or what I had done but for the world and what it had done to him. For his twisted, ruined leg. For the fact that he was home when his brothers were off fighting. For Pa refusing to let him go.

I cried out. I screamed. He stopped. Then he shook me and called me a disobedient little wretch again and let me go. I near fell over, then caught myself.

"Pa should have done that a long time ago," he said.

Then, without another word, he turned. And if Marvelous and I had not followed he would have left us, lost.

Once home, he bade Sam take Marvelous to her house, then he sent me to bed.

"I'm going to tell Ma," I said.

"Have at it" was his only reply.

"Pa would never countenance you hitting me."

"He told me to do whatever I had to do to keep order."

He was secure in his rights. My heart was breaking. This was not my David anymore.

I flung one last charge at him. "What's happened to you?" I appealed.

He lit a cheroot, spit a bit of tobacco off his lip, and eyed me sideways. "I said go to bed."

I went.

Not because I was afraid of him but because I was afraid of what I would say to him if I stayed, what unforgivable things, what words I would never be able to take back once I becalmed myself.

I knew, at fourteen, what he obviously did not know yet at twenty-one. That when you committed an act of meanness to someone you were supposed to love, the angels carried away that act of meanness on the spot and marked it down somewhere forever. And the angels would never be able to give it back, once you were sorry for it.

CHAPTER TWO

I WOKE THAT last Friday in June determined to tell Ma what David had done to me, but when I got down to the kitchen, Josie, our hired girl, already had breakfast on the table and Mama was waiting on me for morning prayers.

"You're late," David said. He was in full mettle, in charge.

I slipped into my chair. Mama was nothing if not intent about prayers, and they were extra long these days because we had to pray for Pa and the boys while the ham and eggs and Josie's fluffy biscuits sat there and waited.

Josie stood by and waited, too, joining in the prayers. She was practically a member of the family. She was a handsome woman, Josie was, only twenty-one, with dark blond hair and blue eyes. She lived alone with her mother, a few streets away. I know she favored my brother David. I often saw her casting admiring glances at him from a distance. But he paid her no mind.

I figured that's what my brother David needed right now. Someone like Josie to take his mind off his anger. And I was waiting for the right moment to tell him that she was smitten with him. If he was too dense to see it himself, someone needed to let him know.

Mama was just asking the Lord for "the Divine favor to watch over our lives and our homes" when two things happened.

First we heard gunshots in the distance. Second, Mr. Hugh Scott, who operated the telegraph office, burst through our front door.

He stood there, out of breath, hat in hand, in the hallway.

David was out of his chair like a shot, grabbing his musket from the corner and going to greet Mr. Scott. "What's happened?" he asked.

"Nothing you'll need that for. Yet," Scott said, pointing to the musket. "And I'm sorry to barge in on you folks, but as a friend of your pa's he'd want me to tell you first."

"What is it?" David demanded.

"Some Confederates have entered town."

"Where?" my brother asked.

"Lower Chambersburg Street, headed toward the square."

David made ready to leave.

"No, David," Mama protested. "Captain Bell has charge of local defense. Isn't he handling it?" She looked at Mr. Scott.

"He is," Scott affirmed. "I just came to inform you. The Rebs are White's Thirty-fifth Virginia Battalion of

Cavalry. They look like a sorry lot. They're badly clothed, screaming, and firing guns into the air, intent on frightening the citizens, is all. They're cursing and petrifying the women. But their officers have given orders for them to capture horses. Myself, I've closed the telegraph office and taken my apparatus to a safe place. I've got to get on now. Be safe, folks."

And in a minute, he was gone.

David saw him out, then stood there. "Damn," he said. "I had Sam take two of our horses to the blacksmith this morning to have them reshod."

"What horses?" I asked. But I knew. You know such things in your bones.

Centipede, Mama's horse. And Ramrod, my own beloved Ramrod.

"I'm sure they'll both be all right," Mama assured him. "Now come back to the table, David. We've still got to eat breakfast. I've asked God to watch over our lives and our homes."

"You should have asked Him to watch over our horses," David grumbled. He secured the front door, came back to the table, and sat down. I noticed that he did not set the musket far from where he was sitting.

Then he raised his coffee cup to his lips and glared at me over it. "You will not go outside the house at all today," he said with quiet sternness, "for any reason."

ALTHOUGH SHE was six years older than I was, Jennie Wade, older sister to pain-in-the-neck Sam, our hired boy, had been my friend for the last two years now. I suppose it was because I had no sisters, because I had three older brothers and dreamed of having an older sister. Jennie filled that empty space in my heart.

She lived half a block away. She had an older married sister, Georgia McClellan, who had just given birth to a baby boy, and she herself was already betrothed to a young man named Johnston Hastings Skelly, who was serving with the Eighty-seventh Pennsylvania Volunteer Infantry.

She had worldwide knowledge already, at the age of twenty, without ever having left Gettysburg. And she taught me things most girls my age did not know and had no way of finding out. I was the wiser for having known Jennie Wade.

We went to lectures together at the college, to concerts, to teas. I helped her sew her trousseau. Of course, David never approved of my close friendship with her, saying she was "too old and worldly" for me by half.

But that was not the whole cloth of the reason. Just part of it. The whole cloth of it was that before his horse had crushed his leg, David and Jennie had been sweethearts, always lolling around together, going to strawberry festivals and church parties and taffy pulls and the like. Always together.

Then, after his horse crushed his leg, she came around less and less. Part of it was David's fault, of course. He did not encourage her to come. He wallowed so in his self-pity, seeing himself as less of a man, and Jennie did not know how to contend with this. She is not one for wallowing, so she finally stopped coming and David never forgave her.

Then, when she and I became friends, he disapproved.

Mama, who only saw good in things, did not object to my friendship with Jennie.

❦

THAT MORNING, following the orders of their officers, the ill-clad and half-in-their-cups men of White's Thirty-fifth Virginia Cavalry charged through town stealing horses. They came upon several young boys leading horses for various and mundane reasons.

One of them was Sam Wade leading Centipede and Ramrod back from the blacksmith. Three men from the Thirty-fifth Virginia had Sam and the horses in tow, and as the procession came past Jennie Wade's house, she came running outside, trailing after them and yelling at the top of her voice.

"Don't you dare take that boy. You release him this minute! Do you hear?"

First they ignored her. Then they laughed at her. Then they said something rude and vile to her.

You did not speak that way to Jennie Wade and live to

tell the world about it. She kept following them and yelling and threatening.

When they came near our house we were all out front, under our giant sycamore tree. I was allowed outside only because I was with Mama and David.

"If the Rebs take our Sam," Jennie shouted at us, "I don't know what I'll do with you folks. I'll hold all of you responsible. I will!"

And she looked directly at me.

"Jennie!" I appealed.

"Quiet," David ordered me.

"You especially," she flung at me.

I dared not open my mouth again.

Mama spoke to the Rebs. "You don't want the boy," she told them. "He's our hired boy."

"No, we don't want the boy," one of the Reb soldiers answered. "You can have him. We are only after the horses."

Sam was shoved back at us, but both Centipede and Ramrod were taken.

I did speak then, not caring what David did to me. "Give me back my horse, you thieves!" I yelled after the Rebel soldiers. I screamed after them. I threw stones. Ramrod reared and cast a wild-eyed look, appealing to me to help her. I knew the look. She was begging.

"Stop it. Can't you see you're only making it worse for her?" David scolded me.

"Well, what am I to do?" I asked him.

"Be quiet is what you do. Behave is what you do. Do as you're told. I'll get them both back. Take Ma inside the house."

While we hadn't been paying mind, Jennie Wade had come over and pulled her brother, Sam, away toward home. "You're not working today," she'd told him. "Come with me."

⁂

LATER THAT MORNING David went to Colonel White of the Thirty-fifth Virginia Battalion to secure the return of our horses. He failed.

The colonel would not return them, not even after David told him that Ramrod was close to the heart of his little sister.

Yes, David told him that. Mama said he did.

What is more, White told David that he had been given the intelligence that we, the Strykers, were a "black abolitionist family." That our family had two sons in the Union army who had "taken much from the South," and so he was taking our horses.

And, David told Mama, when he asked Colonel White where he had gotten his information, he replied that he had gotten it from Jennie Wade herself.

Well, when Mama told me that, I near went out of my wits. "Jennie Wade? My friend?"

"She's no friend of yours," David said. "I always said she was no good for you."

We were at our noon meal. "I'm going over there this afternoon to have it out with her," I said.

"You're not to leave the house without permission," David pronounced. "Especially with those Rebs hanging about. You do, and I'll give you worse than you got last night."

"So give me permission, then."

Mama came alert. She looked at me. "What happened last night?" she asked.

But I just spooned my soup into my mouth and did not answer.

So she persisted. "What happened between you two last night?"

And when again I did not answer, she turned to David. "What did you do to her, David?"

He bit into a muffin. "I whipped her," he said. "She left the house in the dark. Without permission. She went far into the woods. I had to go and fetch her home. I did what I had to do. I'll answer to Pa if you want. I did what I thought was right. I have to keep order around here." He went on eating.

Mama ran her tongue along her lips, eyed her son for a moment, contemplated what he'd told her, and started to speak, then decided against it. Then she looked at me again. "Your brother is the head of the house when your pa is not here. You must obey him," she told me.

"On second thought, I'll not only give permission," David was saying, "I'll accompany you to Jennie Wade's. So you can have your say."

From the kitchen, where she was standing, I saw the look on Josie's face. She was frowning.

"He still loves that Jennie Wade," Josie whispered to me before I left with David.

"No, he doesn't," I promised her. "He doesn't. You must believe me."

And so it was that David walked me over to Jennie Wade's house that afternoon, a walk he had not taken in about six years. He said not a word to me all the way. There was nothing we had to say to each other. Although it would have been nice if he thanked me for not being a tattletale and telling Mama he had whipped me, he didn't. It was something he expected of me, I suppose, some loyalty that harkened back to the old days when we protected each other, would have died for each other.

Once at the Wade house he stayed a discreet distance from her front door, out on the dusty street, and said, "If I see any Rebs, I'll yell for you. If I do I expect you to come immediately."

I agreed and knocked on Jennie's front door. She let me in.

I did not waste time on pleasantries.

"How *could* you have so betrayed our family to Colonel White as to tell him we are black abolitionists?" I demanded.

"Well, aren't you?" She smirked.

"But we never belonged to an abolitionist movement! Pa never belonged to the Underground Railroad! As a matter of fact, as a doctor, he is sworn to help everybody—Northerner or Southerner."

"How sweet. And you don't have two brothers, then, fighting for the Union?"

"Jennie, your betrothed is fighting for the Union! You just wanted to make things difficult for us is all. But why? What did we ever do to you?"

She grimaced. "Truth to tell, I'm sick of you all looking down your uppity noses at me. You Strykers, with all your money, hiring my brother Sam to work for you because you feel sorry for us."

"We thought you wanted Sam to work."

"And I know David doesn't think I'm good enough for you to associate with. You think you're all too good for us."

"So that's it, then. David. It gets back to David, after all."

"Posh, David. A pox on him."

"You still love him—is that it? And you'll never forgive him for turning you away."

"Who does he think he is, with that twisted leg? Can't even fight in the army. Is that something to be proud of?"

I felt myself go hot and prickly all over. "Well, that's enough, as far as I'm concerned, Jennie Wade. You can say all you want about me, but you can't bring low my brother for having a condition he had nothing to do with. We're finished from here on in. Goodbye."

I started out the door.

"Ha!" she called after me. "Heard what that wonderful brother did to you last night. Sam told me. He spanked you. And you, fourteen. And you defend him? You Strykers are all crazier than hooty owls, so there. Good riddance!"

I left. All I could think of, going out the door, was that I was supposed to have been a bridesmaid in her wedding in September. I was supposed to wear pink. The devil with it. I did not like pink anyway.

CHAPTER THREE

ONCE HOME I ran into my room and flung myself onto my bed and cried and cried over my losses this day. The fight with Jennie had undone me. But the loss of Ramrod was deep and searing in my soul.

How could she be gone? What right did the Rebs have to take her? There was no doubt which was the greater loss to me. Jennie would always be about, fighting and standing up for herself. But Ramrod was an innocent animal, taken from her own, unable to speak for herself, wondering why I did not come to rescue her.

She was mine, had been since my brother Joel gave her to me for my eleventh birthday.

We were dear friends, me and that horse. We practically read each other's thoughts, knew each other's needs. What would they do to her?

Would they beat her? Starve her? Lead her into battle, where she would be shot to pieces? She was afraid of gunfire and I'd been careful to keep her clear of it.

Oh, God in heaven, would I never see her again?

The door of my room opened.

"Tacy, come downstairs right now."

David. Intruding on my mourning. "I'm never coming downstairs again."

"You heard me. Ma needs you!"

"I'm going to die up here."

"Not without my permission."

"Your permission be damned."

"Watch your mouth, missy. Ma has some great lye soap that's perfect for washing out dirty little mouths. Anyhow, this is no time for personal pity. We haven't the luxury for it. Now if you don't come, I'm going to come over there and drag you down. Another battalion of Rebs has come into town."

More Rebs! I forced myself up, wiped my face, and went downstairs with him.

And there I beheld a miracle, even though I no longer believed in miracles.

Pa was home! David had tricked me, lied to me! There were no Rebs. There was Pa.

As sure as God made telegraph wires, there he was, my pa, like he'd never left. Sanity returned to us.

He stood there, filling the parlor with his realness in that Union uniform of his, which he hated but which he had to wear. It was full of dust. His hat was off. His gray hair was still full and in need of trimming. His face was tanned and weathered, and those blue eyes still sparkled.

His presence was like a continued conversation.

"Pa!" I shouted.

"Daughter!"

I ran to him, embraced him. He held me in his arms, and in that hug he created the world all over for me, chasing out everything bad that had happened.

I smelled the tobacco on him, the man smells, the horse, the harsh soap, the rum, the medicine smell, the hope and the strength. "Pa"—I pulled back and searched his face—"are you all right?"

There were tears brimming in his eyes. But they would not spill over. He would never let them spill over.

"As right as God's rain, Tacy," he said. "And you?"

"I'm fine, Pa."

"Have you been behaving in my absence?"

I did not answer. I lowered my eyes.

He looked at David for confirmation. "Has she, son?"

"Yes, sir," David lied.

So, David would still protect me. As I had protected him. There was something left between us, then.

Mama's face was wreathed in smiles. "Come," she said. "Josie has a repast laid out in the dining room."

We sat 'round the dining room table for ham and cheese and soup and bread and leftover fish. Pa was starved. He drank four cups of coffee as well as two glasses of Madeira wine.

And he told us what had happened when he came through town on his horse.

"Rebel General Gordon's brigade of infantry was marching through town," he said. "All the citizens were running, frightened. Then General Early came upon our councilman David Kendlehart in front of his home across from the courthouse. A happenstance meeting, but a goodly one. The infantrymen were demanding things—foodstuffs, supplies, clothes, shoes. Early had a list. I was just passing by and Kendlehart bade me take part in the meeting as a witness. Well, what could I do?"

He took a long sip of coffee. We waited.

"Kendlehart said it was impossible for the town to meet the demands on the list. I foresaw break-ins, loot-ings, if we didn't, so I suggested we let the infantrymen examine the merchants' stores and see what they could find. I calculated that by now they'd have stashed away most of their goods."

"A stroke of genius!" Mama clapped her hands.

Pa raised his eyebrows. "Hardly. I just wanted to get home and see my family."

Then we spoke of other things, how the cow was far-ing, how the Rebs had taken the horses, and Pa asked me if people still teased me about my name. I said no. Not lately. They had other things on their mind.

Pa had named me Tacy, and I had taken a fair amount of teasing about it. Because it wasn't a short version of anything. It was just what it was, Tacy. He'd named me after a girl he'd once been in love with, when he was ten years old, back in school in Virginia. She'd died at ten of cholera. And, with Mama's permission, he'd named me after her.

So here I was, Tacy, a name nobody had ever heard of before. And I kind of liked it. "It makes you different,"

David had once told me. That was when David and I had been friends.

When I was excused from the table, I watched out the front window and saw infantrymen passing by, some with piles of hats on their heads. I saw one with a whole bolt of muslin. Did he really need that muslin to keep him warm?

One had spurs attached to his bare feet and another wore a corset around his waist.

Josie came to stand with me for a minute, and we giggled over the sight.

"How did you leave it with Jennie?" she whispered.

"We fought," I whispered back. "She said bad things about David. I stood up for him. We're not friends anymore. And you don't have to worry—he didn't go inside."

At that moment there came a pounding at the kitchen door. She ran to answer it, but David grabbed his musket, stepped in front of her, and motioned her off. He opened it himself.

Marvelous and her mother, Mary, stood there. "Oh, please, let us in," Mary begged.

Mama got up. "Since when do you have to knock? Or ask to be let in?"

David stepped outside to see if there was anyone else about, then ushered them in, locked the door, and shushed everybody. "What's wrong?" he asked Mary in a very low tone.

"We should have left town, our kind. Some of us did.

Those who didn't"—and she had to stop talking to choke back a sob—"were caught by the Rebs, just as we always feared would happen, and lined up early this morning on Chambersburg Street and marched away under guard."

I looked at Marvelous. I could not believe it. She was not looking at me but clinging to her mother like a two-year-old.

Quiet tears were coming down Mary's face. "To the South," she said, "to slavery. We were in that group. Me and Marvelous. My husband, he was at work."

"How did you get away?" David asked.

"The Lord was with us. We slipped away. We come here." Then she did a strange thing. She knelt on the floor. "Oh, please don't send us back. If they come looking for us, don't send us back."

Pa came over then and raised Mary up. "Of course we won't," he said. "Of course we won't. Now come—sit and have a cup of coffee."

"What will we do, Pa?" David asked.

By the time Marvelous and her mother had had their biscuits and ham and coffee, Pa knew, just as he had known how the town would supply the Rebel infantry-men with clothes and supplies.

"I've always thought," he said, slowly and quietly, "that the belfry of the Christ Lutheran Church would be a wonderful place to hide."

It was agreed upon. And it was given to David and me to do the task. Mama hid Mary and Marvelous in our garret until darkness came, and then David and I spirited them away to Christ Lutheran Church on Chambersburg Street and all the way up to the belfry, which was commodious enough to accommodate them, especially with the pillows and blankets Mama had sent along.

"For how long?" Marvelous asked.

"Until this crisis should pass," David told her.

He did not say what crisis. He did not know, nor did I. But I did know that I would come to see them, to keep them supplied with food. We left some with them now.

"It's a heap better than slavery," her mother reminded Marvelous.

I went to bed that night thinking of Marvelous in the belfry of Christ Lutheran Church, and I never thought of Ramrod at all.

❧

PEOPLE LIKE to say that while the Confederates were here they committed no devious acts on us.

Didn't they move seventeen railroad cars a mile out of town during the night and burn them?

Didn't they burn the railroad bridge over Rock Creek?

Weren't the telegraph wires severed?

Didn't they take at least forty darkies, who were free, back south and into slavery?

Didn't they steal my darling horse, Ramrod, away from me?

Didn't they cause a terrible fight between me and my best friend, Jennie Wade?

No trains arrive in town now. No travelers come anymore.

The last of the Rebels who committed no devious acts on us left on Saturday, June twenty-seventh. On Sunday, everyone rejoiced in Gettysburg, saying the town could finally have a peaceful Sabbath as we had always had.

❦

EARLY SUNDAY morning I went up to the belfry of Christ Lutheran Church with David to fetch down Marvelous and her mother, Mary. I had visited them twice, bringing them two meals.

Mary refused to come down. "No, we stay here," she said.

"But the Rebs are gone," David told her. "They left yesterday. All is peaceful now. Come down and have breakfast with us. Ma wants you to."

Mary stood steadfast. "No. They come again. In two days."

Mary sometimes knew things the rest of us did not. Mama said she had "the gift."

"Look," David reasoned. "This morning these bells will ring. You'll be driven out of your head. Come to breakfast. After services you can come back if you wish."

Mary agreed to that.

After services they went back to the belfry.

❦

ON MONDAY MORNING Pa left us, saying he was going to be needed. He had all his doctor's equipment, including his *Physician's Handbook of Practice*.

Pa knew something was about to happen. He had intelligence he could not share. It was why he had come home. But he would not tell us a thing, except that the Union army had a thousand ambulances for duty. He kissed us all, said not to worry. He bade me to be good and to mind David. He said he would be back. Then he mounted his horse and was gone.

On Tuesday, the thirtieth of June, mounted Confederate officers appeared on the crest of Seminary Ridge.

CHAPTER FOUR

EARLY ON TUESDAY morning, the last day of June, Sam came bursting through the back door just as we were about to have breakfast.

"Everyone's coming into the streets!" he told us. He set down the bucket of milk he had in hand. He had just milked our cow, Daisy.

"You ain't listening to me. People all up and down the street are out of their houses," Sam persisted.

"I heard you." David got up, took the milk pail, and set it on the side of the sink. "What for?"

"You mean you don't know?" Sam looked at David as if my brother were the village idiot. "General John Buford's division is coming. Up Taneytown Road. Least six thousand of 'em! Yankees!" He turned to leave.

"Just a minute there!" David's voice halted him.

Sam stopped in his tracks. "Yessir?"

"Where you going? I'm responsible for you while you're here. I can't just let you run off."

I felt a glow of satisfaction, hearing my brother use on Sam the same tone he'd used on me.

"But all the boys are in the streets," Sam protested, "to bring water for the Yankee horses. And the girls"—here he smirked at me—"are bringing the soldiers water, milk, beer, and cake."

"I don't care what others are doing," David said sternly. "Did you finish your morning chores?"

"Yessir."

"Water our horses?"

"You just got one now," Sam reminded him snottily.

David frowned at him warningly. "Don't sass me, boy. I know I just have one. You sass me, I'll take a riding crop to you, and I don't give a tinker's damn what your sister says."

"Sorry, sir. Didn't mean to sass you," Sam said quietly. "I even saddled your horse like you wanted."

David becalmed himself. But why did he want his horse saddled? What was he about this morning?

"Can I go now?" Sam inquired politely. "I won't go far. Just wanna see the Yankees, sir, is all. Be back in an hour."

Satisfied by the submissive tone, David nodded. "Be careful," he warned. "Don't go beyond our street."

Sam was gone before the sentence was finished.

By now, of course, the faint tones of joy that had all along been drifting toward us from outside our windows were distinct sounds of celebration.

I wanted, more than I wanted to take my next breath, to go outside, but I knew better than to ask. Why bother? Only to earn myself a stern no?

But I did give my brother an appealing look, which he was expecting.

There it was, once again in a flash, some of the old harmony between us. We had shared something almost magical once, something I'd never had with either Joel or Brandon, though they were both wonderful brothers to me.

That pleasing agreement of emotion that David and I had enjoyed, that had allowed us to be in tune with each other's needs with no words or warning. It had been something our senses became aware of in an instant.

It happened now.

He knew, without my asking, what I wanted.

"All right," he said, "but you're not to budge from my side."

And so we went out onto the front steps to join the crowds up and down the street who waited the arrival of General John Buford. The Yankees, come to our aid.

They were cavalry, all of them.

David told me that Buford had skirmished of late with Confederate James Longstreet. David kept track of every battle of the war. I don't know where he got his intelligence from, but he also told me that the Confederates who'd come to town were dressed poorly with no shoes on their feet. And the only reason they'd come this way was because they'd heard there was a warehouse hereabouts full of shoes.

He also said that Buford was a cavalry commander who used horses to get his men to where he wanted them to be, then had them dismount to fight.

As they came thundering down the street, young girls,

most of whom I knew, made offerings, tankards of re-freshment. *Water?* I wondered.

Or what? Beer? Buttermilk? The soldiers stopped their horses and accepted the gifts, lifted their hats. Some leaned down from their saddles and kissed the girls' hands. I thrilled at that.

Some girls handed up flowers and started singing "Our Union Forever," and the men tucked flowers in their hats.

Then one officer, leading a brigade, broke away and, seeing David standing there, halted to speak to him.

He asked my brother which was the best way to get out to Chambersburg Pike.

"If you can wait just a second, I'll get my horse. She's saddled," David said. "I'll show you the way."

The officer agreed, and David ran around the side of the house.

So that's why his horse was saddled. So he could be ready for something like this, I thought.

The officer smiled at me. I saw a kind of fondness in his blue eyes as he took my measure and I knew what it was. I knew I was old enough and pretty enough to be appreciated now by a handsome young officer who sported a dashing mustache. In a respectful manner, of course.

My hair, which was of a sandy color, I wore loose to my shoulders most of the time, though Mama preferred me to tie it back, proper-like. My eyes were amber brown. Pa said some man would drown in them someday, but he hoped not too soon, that he hoped my long, fringed eye-lashes would keep him from falling in.

And I was starting to get a figure, finally, at long last.

I smiled back at the officer now, taken not only by the considerable looks of him but by the picture he presented, his sleek horse, the excellent condition of its bridle and halter, the Colt .45 he carried in his holster, the saber he wore.

And in the sling hung from his saddle, the Springfield rifle.

I recognized all his accouterments because Joel and Brandon carried the same things.

"I'm Captain Jensen," he said, and he asked of David, "He your brother?"

"My name's Tacy. Yessir. He's not in the army because of his twisted leg. I have two other brothers serving with the Second Pennsylvania Cavalry. And my pa's a physician with the army. Can I get you some water, sir?"

"That would be nice, Miss Tacy."

So I dashed into the house then and, quick as a rabbit twitches its nose, came out with a sparkling glass of water.

The officer drank it down in one gulp, handed back the glass, wiped his mouth with his sleeve, and thanked me.

Then David came around the side of the house on his horse. "Behave yourself," he admonished sternly.

The officer saw in an instant the connection between us, put his hand to the brim of his hat in a salute, nodded his head, and winked at me.

I wished him good luck. Then he rode off with David. His impatient brigade followed.

In no time at all they were out of sight and lost in the dust that the rest of the cavalry made as they rode down the street.

I was about to go reluctantly back into the house when I heard someone calling me.

"Tacy! Tacy!"

I turned. A girl had broken away from a crowd of people across the street. Nancy Burns. She went to school with me. She lived with her mother and grandfather over on Chambersburg Street. Her pa and older brother were both gone for soldiers.

Nancy's grandfather was from Scotland and said he was descended from the Scottish poet Robert Burns. He told stories about being in the War of 1812 and the Mexican War. He was past seventy now and waiting for the Rebs to come to Gettysburg. He would, he told his family, be ready to fight.

He had tried to enlist but been turned down.

He embarrassed Nancy, because many in town laughed at him. He waited impatiently for an eclipse of the moon. He spoke constantly of fighting. He drank and roamed the town and threw insults at people.

Nancy's mother had her hands full trying to control her father, and so, quite frequently, did not pay mind to what her daughter was about. Now Nancy ran to the stoop of my house.

"Can you come?" She was breathless with excitement,

her face flushed, her golden curls askew. "A few of us are going to the Lutheran Theological Seminary, to the cupola on the roof. I've got my grandfather's binoculars." And she produced them from under the snow white apron she wore over her calico dress.

"You can see near to Washington with this thing. We'll be able to see from there what's happening. Will your brother let you go?"

She had once told me that she was taken aback by David's sternness. And I knew she would not survive two days under his supervision.

"He's not around," I said.

"It's less than a mile from here. Come on—we'll have some sport."

"I should at least tell Mama I'm going to your house or something."

"Good, you do that. Meet us across the street."

So I lied to Mama and told her I was going to Nancy Burns's house for an hour or so. She gave permission and off I went.

The other girls were Debbie Shields, Agnes Bylander, and Virginia Myers. The town was so crowded and the citizens in such a merry mood that no one noticed us walking the half-mile to the end of town, then crossing the street and trekking up the hill to the seminary.

There were by now, if you took the time to look, Yankee soldiers camped all around the base of the hill. You could tell of their presence by the smoke already rising in the air from the many campfires, from the tops of the tents being erected. And then, just when your attention got captured by that, the seminary itself caught and stole your eye.

I'd seen it many times from a distance but had never been up this close. It certainly was a spectacle. It was a huge brick building, three stories high, that seemed to go on and on, standing there against the hard blue sky, with a white cupola on top.

I wondered if there came to be a battle here, if the building would be destroyed.

It had a right to be destroyed, I decided. It was too high-toned for Gettysburg. Those who had built it had been too full of themselves, gotten beyond their own assigned post in life. It frightened me when people did that. It was like, in getting too big for their britches, they were tempting God.

"That," Nancy said, pointing up to the cupola, "is where we're headed."

For a moment it came to me. *She's as crazy as her grandfather.*

We all stared at her, and I knew the other girls were thinking the same thing. We'd come this far. Why not go the rest of the way? And the place seemed deserted since the Rebs had arrived.

"We've got to be careful the Zieglers don't hear us," Nancy cautioned. "Their apartment is on the first floor."

I'd forgotten about them. And I should know better because Mama knew Catherine Ziegler. Her father was the caretaker here. So we crept silently past their door and followed Nancy just as quietly down the wide hall. The sounds of our footfalls echoed anyway as we found our way up the winding stairs, right to the cupola.

Nancy ran right to the end to look out with her binoculars. "Oh my God!" she said. "What a view. You can see everything from here! Oh, girls. You must look!"

One after another we handed the binoculars around. When it came to my turn I was breathless. It wasn't the first time I'd looked through a telescope. Both Brandon and Joel had them, and before they left for war, they had taught me how to use them and trusted me to handle them carefully.

But now, what I saw!

I saw what God must see looking down on us from above.

I saw the mountains, as God must have seen them to His satisfaction, right after He created them, blue and hazy in the west. I saw the men camping on the slopes below us. I could see their faces as they leaned over campfires, the insignias on their uniforms.

I saw one soldier take a locket out of his pocket, open it, and gaze into it to look at a likeness of someone. His sweetheart? His wife?

I felt, truth to tell, like an intruder, looking on things I had no right to see.

I saw a beautiful horse chomping on some oats out of a bag fastened around its neck, and I thought of Ramrod and got sad.

Then I had to give the binoculars back to Nancy.

We all enjoyed a second look around, and then, soon enough, it was time to go.

When we got back downstairs into the wide foyer with the marble floor and the big windows, we stopped.

Just coming in the door was a tall man, a soldier. No, an officer, a very tall and handsome officer.

He had two attendants with him.

He was steely-eyed and wore a handlebar mustache, and he had a good head of hair, for he was young, younger than any officer had a right to be. His uniform had a single row of gold buttons down the front and gold epaulets on the shoulders. He stood stock-still when he saw us. "What are you girls doing here?" he demanded.

His voice was strong and echoed in the empty hall.

We stood, stunned into silence at first. Then I spoke, because I figured that somebody should, lest we all be arrested as spies.

"We were just looking at the countryside with our binoculars, sir," I said.

"Where are you from?"

"We live in town," I said. "I have two brothers serving in the army. My pa is a surgeon in the army."

"What army?"

"Yours, sir. The Union army. My brothers are with the Second Pennsylvania Cavalry."

"What is your name?"

"Tacy Stryker, sir. My brothers are Joel and Brandon Stryker. These are my friends from town, Nancy Burns, Debbie Shields, Agnes Bylander, and Virginia Myers.

Nancy Burns's grandfather is well past seventy now and he's gone off, this very morning, to fight for the Union, General."

"How do you know I'm a general?"

"By your uniform, sir, your epaulets. My brothers, Joel and Brandon, schooled me in a lot of military matters."

He nodded. "I am General John Buford. Those are some of my men out there on the hill. You girls do not belong in this place, and I am very angry to see you here. Do your families know you are here?"

"No, sir," I answered.

"You should be questioned as spies or, at the very least, given a good spanking, but I am going to let you off the hook, because I believe you, Tacy Stryker. Apparently your brothers, being in the military, have schooled you in manners about how to deal with your superiors. Am I correct?"

"Yes, sir."

"Well, they have done a good job, And I wish them well in their future battles. Now go! Go home immediately and stay there. A battle is coming!"

I curtsied. The others didn't. The general nodded at me and smiled as I ran from the room.

Hundreds of Buford's men were strewn about the grounds around the seminary, and I begged Nancy to find another way out than the road down Seminary Hill.

"Why?" she demanded.

"Because I know a captain in the brigade. He stopped by our house this morning for directions, and my brother

David rode off with him to show him the way. If David is still hanging around here and sees me, he'll kill me, that's why. Is that good enough for you?"

It was. We found another path home.

Fortunately, I arrived home before David. And before Mama had cause to worry about me.

But I was on edge the rest of that day, thinking David would find out, praying to God he wouldn't, promising God all kinds of things if only He would keep David from discovering my sins. Even while I longed to tell both Mama and David that I had met General John Buford.

David was in a horrible mood, likely from having seen all those beautiful, capable Yankee soldiers, all those men his own age and younger, who had gone to war. He'd probably been hit in the face with the reality of his deficiency ten times over this morning, like buckets of cold water. And rehashed the unfairness of it on the way home.

Word came to us from Josie that most of the families on the street were inviting Yankee officers into their homes for dinner.

"Did you invite anyone?" Mama asked David.

"No," he answered grouchily from a chair in the parlor, where he was reading the *Lancaster Daily Express*. "I didn't."

"I feel we should," Mama said. "Why don't you take a walk down the street. I'm sure you'll meet an officer. Invite him for supper. Don't you think that would be nice?"

"No, I don't," David responded dully.

I could see Mama's face fall in disappointment. She too suffered from David's moods, though she never said a word about it. She knew she must put up with him, and even respected his moods.

I didn't, though. Never would. "I think you're being rude to Mama," I said.

He looked at me, scowling. "Did I ask what you think?"

"No, but I'm telling you."

"You are, are you? So then, while you're telling me things, tell me where you were today."

My heart came to a standstill. "At Nancy Burns's house. This morning."

There was a moment's dreadful silence. *God,* I prayed, *you're supposed to be on my side, remember?*

My brother was leveling a solemn, searching gaze at me, one of those looks that made me know he was seeing through to my soul. *I'm finished,* I thought. *He knows. Now he's going to swallow me all of a piece, nothing less.*

"Who gave you permission to go out?" he asked.

My voice scarce worked. "Mama did. I asked."

He looked at Mama.

"That's right," she said, "I did."

David lowered his head, went back to his newspaper. "Well, if I'd been home I'd never have given permission."

That was it, that was all. My heart started beating again, and it was so loud that I thought both of them must have heard it.

CHAPTER FIVE

IN SPITE OF his mood, late that night David took me with him to Christ Lutheran Church to bring some vittles to Marvelous and her mother in the belfry.

Oh, it wasn't his idea to take me along. It was Mama's.

"Take her with you, David. She's had a lot of losses these last few days. Her father was home for such a short time and she had to say goodbye to him again. She's still just a little girl, you know, and she misses her father. And she misses Marvelous, too, hidden away as she is up there. And she's lost her horse. And don't forget Jennie Wade. Even though they fought, I know there's an ache in her heart for Jennie."

Tears built up in my throat when Mama said all that.

She had summed up my troubles before I could even acknowledge them to myself. And even though she understood and respected David's moods, he was still her son, and on occasion she could still reprimand him.

And on occasion he listened.

He stood there in the kitchen with a lantern in one hand and a basket of food in the other.

"All right," he said to me, "come on, then. But I'm

doing this for Mama." He handed the basket of food to me and picked up a stone jar of water. "And we leave when I say so."

❦

WE FOUND our way through the darkened church and up the stairs with no difficulty.

Marvelous had seen us coming and was waiting excitedly. We hugged.

"I know this whole place by heart," she said. "I know how many pews there be and I tiptoe around up and down between the aisles at night when nobody's about."

Her mother was busy thanking David for the food and water, asking him the news and complaining how she could not keep her daughter in tow. "Awful difficult keepin' that chile quiet in here," she was saying. "An' I miss my Basil so. Did you get word to him that we's okay, David?"

"Yes," my brother told her. "He wanted to come and see you, then decided he didn't want to let on to anybody that you're still in town. You know you and Marvelous could come and hide out in our cellar, Mary."

"Nosir, don't wanna get you all in trouble. We stayin' right here till this thing blow over. I do anythin', anythin' to keep me an' Marvelous from bein' sold into slavery. Oh, this food is so good. Tell your mama thank you. She is such a good woman. And you, son"—she put her hand on his arm—"you be such a good boy. I always did love you, David, like a son."

They ate the food and I sat next to Marvelous in near silent companionship, talking only occasionally, telling her how I missed her, making plans for what we'd do when the Rebs were driven out of town. We giggled, we whispered. David and Mary paid no mind to us, and by the lantern's light we near fell asleep, leaning against each other while David and Mary exchanged news and confidences.

Then David was shaking me. I had fallen asleep. "Time to go," he said.

"Oh, can't she stay the night?" Marvelous begged.

I had wanted to ask, but dared not.

David was kindly to Marvelous. "No, sweetie," he said, "I'm afraid not. You and your mother might have to flee on a moment's notice. Your mother and I have discussed what she should do if this happens. You'll see Tacy soon, I promise. This will all be over in a few days. The Yankee army is here and it's very strong. They'll drive the Rebs out of town. Now go to sleep."

He grabbed my hand and drew me to my feet, then took a blanket from Mary and covered Marvelous in a manner so tender that I gazed in amazement. *This is my old brother David,* I thought.

Then he led me downstairs and we went out into the night.

He said not a word to me all the way home.

I had always known that David cared about Marvelous and her mother. He hated the very idea of slavery, and while my brothers Joel and Brandon may have gone off to war to save the Union, I think David wanted to go off to free the slaves.

We never discussed it as a family. Pa never intruded on his sons' private reasons for going to war, never tried to influence them. He always allowed them to make up their own minds about politics and such. But I know for a fact that David hated slavery.

❦

WHEN WE GOT home, the houses on the street were dark, with the exception of a few that still had lights burning in some of the windows.

Mama had left a lantern aglow in a front window for us. We saw it from a distance. But as we neared the house we saw a figure huddled on our stoop.

As we approached, David put an arm out to hold me back and walked on ahead. He didn't have his musket with him, but shoved in his waistband in back of his trousers he had a Colt .45. "Can I help you, sir?" I heard him ask.

The man was leaning forward, his elbows on his knees, his head in his hands. At his feet was a knapsack. In the light of David's lantern, I saw his gray hair under an old cap. And I recognized him in an instant.

I stepped forward. "That's Mr. Cameron," I told David. "From over to York Street. He's near ninety years old!"

"Stay back," David said. Then to Mr. Cameron, "Can I help you, sir? Are you lost? Can I help you find your way home?"

Mr. Cameron raised his eyes to my brother. "I know the way home, son. I'm not dotty. I just don't wanna go there. I live alone now and I'm scairt what with the Rebels in town and the war comin' here and all. I know your pa, the doctor, and I was wonderin' if you'd be so kind as to let me stay in your cellar for a few days, until the Rebs are gone. I'd be no trouble. Don't eat much at my age. Just need a blanket and a corner and some coffee. I do like my coffee. What say you, boy?"

Mr. Cameron saw me standing a bit behind David and smiled. "Nice little girl you got there."

"She's my sister," David said. "As I recollect, you have a son, don't you, Mr. Cameron?"

The face of the old man, which looked like a map of Gettysburg hastily drawn by a Union officer, went sad. "Yes, I do. He's in the army. Somewhere. Don't know where. Don't know which army. Haven't seen him in ten years. Don't expect to see him in ten more. What say you, now? Think your ma would let me in?"

David nodded. He went up the stoop, helped old Mr. Cameron to his feet, and guided him through the door.

I followed.

David locked the door behind us, held Mr. Cameron by the arm, then set him down in a chair. He told me to fetch a warm blanket. I did so. Then he bade me find some coffee on the stove in the kitchen. There was always coffee on the stove in the kitchen. I poured some into a cup, put some sugar in it, and brought it to Mr. Cameron, who accepted it gratefully.

Then David ordered me to bed.

As I was going up the stairs, I looked over the banister.

David was guiding Mr. Cameron down to the cellar, with the blanket in one hand and his other around Mr. Cameron's shoulder. The old man was still holding his cup of coffee.

I lay awake for a while staring at the ceiling, thinking of Marvelous sleeping under the blanket David had so tenderly wrapped around her in the church belfry, so high up, and Mr. Cameron sleeping under the blanket David had wrapped around him in a corner of our cellar, so far down.

The thought gave me a sense of comfort. And then I minded Pa, wondering where he was sleeping tonight. And *if* he was sleeping. And my mind wandered to my horse, Ramrod. Was she resting on warm, sweet hay, with her stomach filled with oats? Or was she starving someplace on some rough terrain, with scratches on her, and scars from some soldier's rough spurs, thinking of me and waiting for me to come and rescue her?

"God does not visit us with troubles we do not have the strength to survive," Jennie Wade used to tell me. She said that thought used to get her through the bad times.

Were these bad times for her now? Did she grieve over

the fight we'd had as I did? Was she sorry? Did she miss our friendship? At the end of the day when Sam came home, did she ask him what had gone on at our house?

I knew she still loved David. How could she even think of marrying another man when she still loved David? Was part of my brother's bitterness born out of the fact that he, too, still loved Jennie?

Could I keep my own counsel and not tell David that Jennie still loved him? Did I have the obligation to tell him that? Didn't my loyalty belong to Josie, whose love was not fickle?

I cried myself to sleep.

❧

IN THE MORNING I was hurled awake by the sound of gunfire.

I jumped out of bed, threw on my clothes, and ran downstairs.

Again, from the front windows, I saw people coming out of their homes all up and down the street. Josie was setting the table for breakfast. David was out back, yelling at Sam for something. Mama was with him.

Immediately, I went out on the front stoop.

"They're fighting," Mrs. Broadhead yelled at me from her front stoop across the street. "They're starting to kill each other!"

I could see soldiers up at the end of our street, in

bunches, could hear the sound of musketry, dogs going crazy with frenzied barking, the whinnying of horses.

"Well, that's what they've come for, isn't it?" David's voice, behind me. His hands roughly gripping my shoulders and pulling me inside. "To kill each other?"

He yelled it across the street at Mrs. Broadhead as he pulled me inside, then slammed and locked the door.

THE FACT WAS, our cow was gone.

Daisy, the sweetest creature known to mankind, after my Ramrod, had been stolen in the night by some demonic Rebel who'd come sneaking about.

That was what David had been scolding Sam for outside when I'd come down this morning. Sam had taken the brunt of it.

He'd neglected to lock the barn door.

"It isn't as if," Mama said at breakfast, once she'd stopped crying about Daisy, "the Rebs couldn't have broken through the lock and taken her anyway, David."

David was adamant. Once he laid blame it stayed on the accused. For the rest of your born days. "Yes, but it would have made too much noise, them breaking in. This way it was easy for them. It makes me madder 'n hell making things easy for them."

"We've got to get a dog," I said. We hadn't had a dog since our Beau died, half a year ago now. He was all the dog we'd needed, a faithful watchdog, companion, and friend. He'd been fifteen and died of old age. "Pa said we could get another one," I reminded my brother.

"This isn't the time," he told me. "Not yet."

This is exactly the time, I wanted to snap back. Instead I said, "Do you think the Rebs will use Daisy for milk? Or kill her for meat?"

The minute the words were out of my mouth I wished I could reach out and grab them back. Mama broke into a new freshet of crying.

David slapped his hand down on the table. "Did you *have* to say that?"

"I'm sorry, no. I'm sorry, Mama." I got up and hugged her around the shoulders. "I'm sure they need fresh milk more than anything. Please don't cry."

A knock came on the front door then, thankfully, distracting Mama. Josie started forward to answer it, but David intercepted her. With his musket in hand.

It was Nancy Burns.

"Hello, Nancy." My brother let her in and my heart leaped inside me for a second, hoping she'd say nothing about our adventure yesterday. Then I becalmed myself. No, she wouldn't. She was more frightened of David than she'd likely be of God on Judgment Day.

"You shouldn't be out and about," David admonished her gently. "The battle is starting."

"Yessir, I know. But I just came to say that my grandpa . . . he, well he's going off to fight. And my mama can't stop him!" She was starting to get tears in her eyes, and her voice broke as she looked up at David.

"So he's really doing it, is he?" David asked. His own voice was husky, which meant he was allowing feelings to creep into it, something he rarely did.

"Yessir, and he's going to get killed. And we don't know what to do."

We all watched in fascination as David put his hands on Nancy's shoulders, then gently said in the softest of voices, "Listen to me, child. Did you ever think of this? That if your grandpa doesn't go off to fight today as he so desperately wants to, that if he stands by and lets others go, that act alone may kill him?"

Nancy stood there round-eyed, considering the possibility of it. The thought had never occurred to her. Or to any of us.

But it had to David.

Slowly, Nancy ingested the thought and nodded her head. "I'll tell my mama that," she said. "Thank you, sir." She turned to go, but David restrained her.

"I'll accompany you," he told her. "I'll see you safely home."

❦

When he returned about ten minutes later, none of us said anything. But at breakfast when he didn't know I was looking at him, I stole glances at my brother. He'd gone right back to his surly, silent mood, and as I furtively studied him, I minded that the way he'd been with Nancy now, and with Marvelous and Mr. Cameron last night, was the way he used to be with me.

But he was two people now. He had a bad side and a good side. And he reserved the bad side for me. It broke my heart, realizing that. But for his sake, I was glad there was some of the good side left in him, at least.

After breakfast he took food down to Mr. Cameron, and made several trips up and down, attending to him. The man would not come above stairs. I even saw him taking him up the outside cellar stairs to the outhouse, then back down again, and instructing Josie to feed him about noon.

Up until now, the sounds of fighting had been far off, and looking out the windows, it seemed to me as if people were going about their regular lives. Some had already climbed onto the roofs of their houses. I saw men and boys walk toward the west of town. Then I felt David standing behind me.

"Where are they going?" I asked.

"To the ridges, to see the action," he said.

We heard bugle calls in the distance and then, about nine o'clock, a terrible, resounding boom.

"Cannon," David said.

Then more awful, awful noise that violated the soul.

"Artillery," David told me. "The Confederates on Herr's Ridge must be firing at the Union men near McPherson's Ridge."

How did he know so much? Then I remembered,

he'd spent much of the day with the Union army yesterday.

In a short time the civilians from town who'd gone to see the battle came running back, and soon stray shells and bullets were finding their way into town. People were coming down from the rooftops. David pulled me away from the window.

"No telling where a stray missile will strike," he said.

The last sight I saw was a Union general and his staff riding down our street. "Are they retreating?" I asked David. But he was no longer communicating with me. He had gone inside of himself, and all he said was "Stay away from the windows."

The crashing of shells increased steadily outside as the morning progressed. Mama took to baking bread with Josie. Soon the house was filled with the delicious aroma, and I wandered, fidgeting. David went about securing windows and doors, closing the shutters.

A courier came galloping up and down the street, shouting something.

David opened the front door. I heard him exchange brief words with the man. He came back in, crestfallen. "Our General Reynolds was killed this morning," he told us.

Mama turned from the kitchen table where she was kneading bread. "Oh, not John!" she wailed. "I always felt as if I knew him! Your father wrote of him frequently in his letters home. They became such good friends at Antietam and Chancellorsville! Everyone respected Reynolds so!"

"I'm sorry, Mama," David said. "I know Reynolds arrived here early this morning and led his infantry right into battle. The courier said he turned in his saddle to look for more troops and just fell right to the ground, from a bullet in the back of his neck."

Mama wiped a tear from the corner of her eye with the back of a flour-covered hand, nodded, and went right back to kneading her bread. "That other loaf must be done. Take it out of the oven, Josie."

"I only wish I'd had the honor of meeting him," she said.

"Tacy, go help your mother," David told me.

I did so, losing myself in the mess of butter and flour and other ingredients, near jumping out of my skin as every shell that crashed seemed closer to us, as the realization that the sound of wagon wheels outside were not civilians on a jaunt but ambulances bringing wounded to town.

David told us that, offhandedly. "Wounded coming," he said, the way one would announce that it had started to rain. Then he went out to the barn.

Taking advantage of his absence, I ran to the window, my hands covered in flour. I had to see. But the first wounded I saw was not in an ambulance. It was a man on a beautiful black horse, the kind a prince rides in a fairy tale. But this was no prince. It was Mr. Emil Watts, who ran one of the grocery stores in town. And he had, lying across his horse, a soldier with blood pouring out of one leg of his trouser, right down the side of the beautiful black horse.

Mr. Watts stopped in front of the house of Mrs. Broadhead, who sometimes helped in his store.

I opened the window to hear.

"Emily," he shouted. "Emily, come out here. You've got to help with this man!"

She came out, Mrs. Broadhead did. She stood there, hands on hips. "What do you want me to do, Emil? I'm not a doctor!"

"I want you to be a human being, is what I want!" he said. "I want you to take him in and help me mend him."

Together they carried the man inside.

And then scores of wounded came, some dragging themselves, some being led by comrades, supported by comrades, piled into ambulances, and holding on to horses.

They had gaping wounds, gashes, bloodied clothes, partial limbs. Some had hideous faces, some could not see. Blood flowed from parts of their bodies they did not even know they had.

Some cried for their mamas. Others just whimpered, while some did not seem to know where they were or who they were or, worse yet, why they were.

Girls and women lined the streets, handing them cups of water.

I heard the regimental band playing patriotic tunes.

They played "Dixie," of all things. And "The Star-Spangled Banner."

David must have come in from out back. Before I knew what was happening, he was jerking me away, shaking me, and closing the window and shutters.

"I told you to stay away from the windows, didn't I?"

"The men are bleeding, David," I told him.

"Everyone's bleeding," he said.

So I went back to my stupid bread making. *Who is all this bread for, anyway?* I wanted to ask. But I dared not.

Around noon we heard a shell hit a roof. I knew immediately what roof it was. And I knew I was not mistaken.

It was the roof of Christ Lutheran Church.

And what was on the roof but the belfry.

We all just stared at each other for a second, because the others knew it, too. I had a lump of dough in my hand. I'd been just about to knead it, and now I squeezed it unmercifully and I yelled.

"The church!" I yelled. "The belfry! They've been hit! Marvelous has been hit! And Mary!" I dropped the roll of dough, flung off my apron, and ran from the kitchen into the hall.

"Stop!" David ordered. "Where do you think you're going?"

But he was no more than a cricket on the hearth to me now. His words held no power over me. I did not care what he said, what he did to me. My breath was coming in quick spurts. I could scarce breathe. Tears for what I already knew had happened flowed down my face. Hysterics took over and I welcomed them. Hysterics, after all, were the order of the day.

"I'm going to find my friends," I spit out at him. "'Cause they're dead. And they need me." I could not stop my crying. I did not especially care to.

I opened the front door to go out. All was chaos on the street. Good. I was ready for it, in tune with it. Inside all was darkness for me now.

Then I felt David's hands on my shoulders. Not rough, but gentle, as he turned me to face him. "Tacy," he said softly. "Tacy."

I heard him from very far away, his voice cutting through the darkness like a beam of light.

He kept saying my name like that, softly, so that I followed the sound of it, like I was lost and finding my way home.

Then, of a sudden, I felt myself drawn to him, his arms around me tenderly, holding me close until my face was against his shirt front, until I could smell the shaving soap he used and the tobacco and, yes, even the rum and the scent of his horse, and I could hear the beating of his heart, something alive and hopeful.

He held me like that for a while. "It's all right," he said gently. "I'm here. I'm going to take care of you. I'll make it all right."

I came home. I believed him. I felt the calm overtake me and I quieted down.

I looked up at him and nodded. "I'm sorry," I said.

I was back and he knew it. He nodded solemnly. "You're allowed. Doesn't mean I'm never going to scold you again, though." He twitched my nose.

Had I really seen something in him, some kindness directed toward me to give me hope, then? Would I see it again? Or was it a flame, briefly ignited and now gone out?

"Now, I'm going to take you over to the church. I'm sure they're both all right. But you must be brave. Promise me."

I promised. And we went to the church together.

CHAPTER SIX

WE COULD SEE, before we got to the church, that the belfry was destroyed and that there was considerable damage to the roof. I drew in a deep breath, seeing it, but that was all. Then, as we got to the side door, there were all kinds of people about.

Civilian men were dragging away fallen pieces of the roof to make way for the military carrying in litters of wounded soldiers.

And women, most of whom we knew, were carrying in stacks of linen, blankets, and bandages, pitchers of water and basins.

David and I just stood there, open-mouthed at the spectacle. We saw Emily Broadhead. She had on a bloodstained apron. Her hair was bound with a white kerchief.

"Is anybody dead inside?" David asked.

"Not yet," she answered. "The doctors aren't allowing it."

Doctors. "Is my pa in there?" I appealed.

"No, honey. Not here. But far's I know there are plenty of other makeshift hospitals being set up in town. He might be in one of those. Now I've got to run home a minute." And she was gone.

We were about to enter the side door she'd just come out of when it seemed filled of a sudden. Because the person who stood there filled my eyes.

Jennie Wade was standing there.

She wore an apron, but there was no blood on it so I calculated she'd just brought some supplies.

She just waited there for what seemed like the length that a full moon hung around, staring at David. She said nothing.

"Hello, Jennie," David said.

Her eyes sought his. It was as if I did not exist. And I thought, *Why don't you say something, Jennie?* And then I thought, *Why don't I say something to her?* We'd been friends for years. Killing was going on all around us. Men were bleeding inside, crying. Houses all around us were being shelled. And here we were, two old friends, and we couldn't even say hey to each other.

She just nodded at David and ran out of the doorway right past us, as if a Confederate were chasing her with a bayonet.

David said nothing. We went inside.

All was organized confusion. Some men were on the floor. Still others in the main vestry. There was an amputating bench in an anteroom that opened off the main hall, and we heard yells of pain coming from within. Doctors were operating right there, with local women serving as nurses.

People were rushing around answering the call of the wounded, bending over them, giving them water and tending their wounds, listening to their words, comforting them.

This, I thought, *must be what the first room of hell looks like, where they decide which room you go to next.*

Looking around we saw no Marvelous, no Mary. David led me upstairs to the auditorium. Here most of the wounded were laid out, from one end of the room to the other, a few on cots, most on blankets on the floor, a few lucky ones on mattresses.

It took us both a few brain-frying seconds to adjust our eyes to the scene. *All these men, wounded just this morning.* And the woman downstairs had told us there were more hospitals in town.

And then, oh glorious then, I sighted across the wide expanse of pews Marvelous and her mother.

They were doing the same thing as the other women. They were aiding the wounded soldiers.

I tugged David's sleeve and he looked down at me and nodded, for he'd seen them, too.

"Can I go to them?" I asked.

"Yes, but just to say hello. And ask where they're staying tonight. They can sleep in our cellar, if they still need to hide. I'm going to make sure Joel and Brandon aren't here."

I quickly made my way around and through the people, stepping over wounded, even stopping once to give a young man some water. Looking back once, I saw David wandering around, searching, offering help to some of the soldiers as he inspected the faces.

When I caught up with Marvelous and her mother,

Marvelous screamed briefly, then covered her mouth, re-membering where she was. We hugged, we cried.

"We were so lucky," she told me. "The wounded started coming in before the belfry got hit. And me and Mama came down, right off, to help. So we weren't up there when the shell came. Else we'd be dead."

I hugged her again, tears streaming down my face.

"The angels were with us," her mama said.

I invited them to our house, to hide in our cellar. "No, we stay right here," her mama insisted. "We stay with the wounded."

"But suppose the Reb soldiers come and take you?" I asked.

Another woman standing nearby, who introduced her-self as Mrs. Jacobs, interrupted our conversation. "I'd like to see that happen," she said vehemently. "I'd like to see a Reb soldier walk through that door and take these two won-derful people with him and walk out alive to tell the tale! They have nothing to worry about. They are part of us."

I thanked her, then I saw David signaling to me from across the auditorium. "I must go," I told them sadly. "Send word if you need us."

And I ran toward David with tears still streaming down my face.

❧

WE WENT BACK downstairs and he made a tour of the wounded there, too, lest any be Brandon or Joel. None was. We headed home and in the street men in gray uniforms with bayonets fastened to their rifles were chasing retreating men in blue, who turned to face them down. I was dumbfounded as I saw a Yankee spear the shirt front of a Reb, then saw the Confederate's blood spurt out and spread all over both of them.

"How will we get home?" I asked David tearfully.

He took my arm and we turned from the street. "We'll get there. Come on—you shouldn't see this." And soon we were skirting through alleys, around the backs of houses, ducking through fences and behind outhouses and sheds and copses of trees.

David is a cripple in the true sense of the word. The army turned him down for a cripple, because he drags his leg. But after you know him awhile, you do not even take heed of it. And if he wants, he can drag that leg so fast, he can almost run.

So now we almost ran. My skirt caught on a fence and ripped as David lifted me over it. A shell burst overhead. We heard a command issued from out on the street.

"I said shoot, damn it!" Then a shot, a yell, and silence. And someone died.

Finally we came to the fence that encircled our property. David took a quick look around, crouched down, and said we should make an almost-run for the back door. We made it inside, an accomplishment of the highest order.

In all the confusion, in all the distraction of the carnage in the streets, in all our attempts to just survive, I had forgotten to tell him the one thing I wanted to tell him on the way home.

David, you should know, Josie is positively smitten with you.

Then we were through the back door and into the kitchen. It was full of people. Soldiers. All ours. Josie was serving hot coffee. Mama was slicing fresh bread. There were dishes of butter and cheese on the table and a side of ham.

One of the younger officers was eyeing Josie flirtatiously.

And immediately I saw, to my satisfaction, that David, my stone-hearted brother David, was jealous!

There was Josie, pouring some coffee for a young officer, who was nothing if not handsome, and he standing over her so close that if he were any closer he'd be in the pot, his eyes going over Josie salaciously. Well, David stepped forward, put his hand on Josie's shoulder possessively, and gave her a peck on the cheek! "Got some for me, Josie?" he said.

Immediately, the young officer took his cup of coffee and moved away.

Josie blushed and handed David a cup of coffee. I thought I'd faint when he winked at her, then moved toward Mama to report about Marvelous and Mary. I was reaching for a piece of buttered bread when another young lieutenant asked if I lived here.

"Yes, sir."

"Name's Lieutenant Stover. I'd like to give you this."
And from behind him he drew a sword with an elegant
hilt. "I took it just this morning from a Confederate officer I captured. Don't want to lose it. Can I leave it here
with you, miss? Will you keep it for me?"

"Of course I will. I'd be honored to. My name is Tacy,"
I said.

He nodded respectfully. "If," he said shyly, and then
he faltered and had to start again, "if I don't come back
for it, means I've fallen in battle. If that happens, I leave
it to you."

Our eyes met. His were deep and brown and sad.
Then he nodded, asking me to seal the agreement. And I
nodded back, sealing it.

Satisfied, he compressed his lips and handed the
sword over.

It was heavy and I handled it respectfully, nodding
again.

He turned away. "Got to get back to battle," he said.
"Our men out there need me."

Then he was gone.

The other officers took their leave shortly after,
thanking Mama for the food, all saying the same thing—
they had to get back to the battle, the men out there
needed them.

David left, too, telling Mama he was going to look for
Pa, that the officers had told him where many of the
makeshift hospitals were. There were at least ten others in
town, he said.

"Be careful on the streets, David," Mama begged.

He kissed her. "Not going on the streets," he said.

I knew he was also going to look for Joel and Brandon. "Don't worry about him, Mama," I told her. "He knows his way around these streets and alleys like a ferret."

❦

I STAYED AWAY from the windows the rest of that afternoon as I knew David wanted me to, and I helped Mama and Josie clean up the kitchen. All the while the sounds of fighting came to us from the street outside. Horrendous sounds.

Mama was beginning to look a little weary around the edges, so I suggested she go upstairs and take a nap.

"With this going on?" she asked. "I'll not go upstairs, I'll tell you that. Who knows but a shell will hit the roof."

"I'm sorry—it was a bad suggestion," I said. "Here, why don't you sit in this chair." It was Pa's, his most comfortable one. I pushed it close to a wall and picked up his favorite comforter. "I'll wrap this around you, Mama. You don't have to sleep. Just wrap it around you and sit, like Pa used to do."

I raised a corner of it to my face. "It even smells of Pa," I tempted her. "Of his pipe tobacco and such."

Her eyes twinkled in spite of herself. "You're a little devil, Tacy," she scolded. But she crossed the room, took the comforter from me, and settled down in the chair. I wrapped it around her and in two minutes her eyes were closed. Despite all the noise from outside, she soon was asleep.

Within half an hour there was a knock on the back door. Josie and I looked at each other. Not wanting more knocking to wake Mama, I crept to the door, pushed aside the checkered curtain, and peered out.

It was a Yankee soldier, apparently not wounded but definitely the worse for wear. I opened the door a crack. "Can I help you?" I asked.

He wore at least two days' worth of beard, and there were wrinkles at the corners of his eyes. He looked considerably older than David. I would not put the word *disreputable* to him, but his clothes were long past shabby. Still, some men carried that air of shabbiness, even in good clothes. I suspected he was one of them. But he was one of ours, so I listened to him.

"I'm looking for my pa," he said.

"The officers are all gone. They left."

"No, miss, you don't understand. I live hereabouts. At least I used to once, long time past. I went home to find my pa. People said he came over here to hide."

Something clicked inside my head, where things click when your brain finally decides to stop being stupid. "What's your name?" I asked.

"Michael Cameron. Haven't seen my pa in ten years."

I opened the door and let him in. "He's down in the cellar," I said.

I warned him to be quiet under pain of banishment, that my mama was sleeping, and he obeyed. I led him downstairs to the cellar.

We found Mr. Cameron fast asleep on some straw in a corner, covered by a blanket, his empty dish from lunch and his drained-dry coffee cup next to him.

Michael Cameron just stood there, leaning on his rifle, staring at his father in silence. "Damn, he got old," he whispered.

"People do," I returned in my own whisper.

He nodded his head. He ran a hand over his face. He continued to stare.

"Don't you want to wake him and say hello?" I asked.

He didn't answer right off. When he did, he just shook his head no.

I could not believe it. I continued to look fixedly at the man as if he were demented. *You haven't seen your father in ten years and you go through the trouble to stop by and don't even want to wake him and say hello?*

But I said nothing. What could I say? *And I thought my family was confused!*

"You want, you can come back later," I told him in the same whispery voice.

"No, I gotta catch up with my unit. Tell me, you got any pencil and paper?"

"Sure." Quiet as I could be, I rummaged about. We had everything down here in the cellar, although I don't know why I accommodated him. I found paper and pencil and he held it against a box and wrote a quick note, then folded it in half and leaned over his father and tucked it in the lapel of his jacket.

Then he took one long last look and we went upstairs while Mr. Cameron went right on sleeping.

I offered Michael some leftover coffee. No, he said. Some bread and butter and ham? No. Some water, then? No. He was antsy; he had to go. He thanked me, and before I knew what was happening, he was gone out the back door.

I minded what he was about after he left.

He was afraid his father might wake while he was still here. And he would have to meet him. He wanted to be gone.

After he left, I thought about my own pa and wondered if I'd ever see him again.

I wondered how Michael Cameron could stand over his father and not want to wake him, to hug him. Whatever could have happened between them that, with his father so old and with such an awful war going on right outside our door, a war in which Michael might be shot to death just going down the street, he couldn't have woke his pa and hugged him?

I decided I knew nothing at all anymore. Nothing.

I threw myself down on the settle and cried into the pillows so Mama would not hear me. I stayed like that, face in the pillows, until David came home.

CHAPTER SEVEN

SOMEONE WAS SHAKING my shoulder, waking me.

"Tacy, Tacy, wake up. We have to eat supper."

Supper? Isn't it too late? What time is it? I opened my eyes, expecting to see darkness, surprised to see light, but not surprised to hear the gunfire outside.

Mama was leaning over me. I smelled the supper, meat and onions. David stood behind her. He looked disheveled, and he was frowning.

"What happened?" he asked.

"Nothing." I rubbed my eyes, trying to bring my senses forward. "I fell asleep."

"Josie said you fell asleep crying. What happened?" he asked again. "Who was that man who was here?"

There was nothing for it. I had to tell him. "Michael Cameron. Mr. Cameron's son."

Both his and Mama's eyes widened as we sat down at the table.

"You don't say." David rubbed his hands and reached for the wine bottle. "So he finally came to see his father. Well, what did Mr. Cameron have to say? Josie?" He looked up at her as she set a bowl of mashed potatoes down in front of him. "You brought him down his supper. Was he happy?"

Josie shook her head. "Didn't say a word, Mr. David. Not a word. Yes, I brought him down his supper, but he was still sleeping. Never saw a man sleep so much in all my born days."

David frowned. "He's all right, isn't he?"

She went back into the kitchen to fetch a bowl of beans. "He isn't dead, if that's what you mean." Josie was plainspoken. She wasted no words, and quite frankly it was refreshing. "I'll have another try at bringing him some supper soon."

She came back with the bowl of beans in one hand and a platter of meat in the other. As David stood to carve the meat, she took a moment to give me a meaningful look, and I met her eyes and blushed.

I knew what it was for. *If you're going to tell him what happened, don't do it till after supper. I don't want this excellent meal I cooked ruined. 'Cause I know your brother, and if you tell him, there'll be all kinds of hell to pay.*

That's what the look said. Josie knew all about what had transpired between me and Michael Cameron. She'd heard it all, hadn't she?

Then she went back into the kitchen to get the gravy and bread. And we ate.

As we ate, David told Mama that he was unable to locate Pa, that other doctors had told him Pa was working in a field hospital and told them that he'd never seen so many wounded.

"Some good news, though," he told us. "I ran into Mrs. Burns, coming home. She was returning from the courthouse. Come back from seeing her father. He was being treated there."

Mama's hand flew to her mouth. "He fought, then? He was wounded?"

David smiled. "With the One Hundred and Fiftieth Pennsylvania Volunteers. She said they called him 'Daddy' but he didn't care. He grabbed a musket off a wounded man and went at it. He shot a Confederate officer off his horse and they cheered him. He got hit with a bullet on his belt buckle and the shot doubled him over. Then he got hit on his ankle and a Confederate doctor treated him."

We listened, fascinated, and I was glad for Nancy. Maybe now her grandpa wouldn't be laughed at anymore.

There was chocolate cake for dessert. We lingered, in spite of the gunfire outside, over coffee and cake. I saw Mama tremble several times, saw David frown as if to say, *What's this? Is it finally getting the best of you, Mama? Should I have sent you away to your sister's in Philadelphia?*

After dessert, as we stood, trying to determine if it was safe enough to spend the evening in the parlor or if we must go to the cellar, I told David I had to speak with him.

He understood the look on my face and nodded silently. We went into Pa's study.

David closed the door, expecting anything. I got right to it.

"When you go down to see Mr. Cameron, you're going to find a note on his lapel," I told him.

He scowled. "Explain."

"His son wrote it and left it for his pa."

He nodded his head slowly, his eyes narrowing. David was nothing if not wise. "His pa was sleeping and he did not wake him," he said dully.

"Yes."

He cursed. Nobody could curse like David. It was never in anger, always done softly and carefully, almost like a prayer. I think God must have taken it as one, because—and I hope this is not blasphemy—God's name was somehow always in it.

Silence between us for a moment while I waited to see where he was going to lay blame. Likely on me.

I was right. "You were there with him."

"Yes."

"You gave him the paper and pencil for the note?"

"Yes."

"Why didn't *you* wake Mr. Cameron?"

I'd asked myself that a hundred times since Michael had left. I'd asked myself in my sleep. "I don't know, David. I thought about it, but I didn't know if I had the right to."

"The *right? The right?* You had the *obligation!* That man's father is in our house. We are caring for him. And that is part of caring for him. Seeing after his interests. God, Tacy, don't you have any sense at all? I thought that sooner or later you'd acquire some, unselfconsciously, at least, just absorb it like a flower absorbs the sun!"

I started to choke back tears.

"No crying. I won't have it! Come along with me."

I ceased crying before it even started. The tears were scared out of me. I followed him out of Pa's study, down the hall, and past Mama and Josie, then down the cellar stairs. There we found Mr. Cameron, still sleeping. We stood over him just half a second.

Then David reached down and gently took the note from him.

"David, no!" I whispered.

His scowl was so fierce that all it needed was black powder to wound me in the head.

He gave the note to me. "Don't read it," he directed. "Rip it up."

"But, David, we have no right!"

"We have no right to let him have it and break his heart. Or maybe kill him on the spot. Now rip it up."

I did so. Then he took the pieces and, for good measure, threw them in the fire that burned in the cellar hearth.

"Tell this to nobody," he said.

I could not believe what we had just done. What I had just done at his bidding. Of course, I had no choice: I *had* to do his bidding. I had to obey him. Mama herself had told me that.

But how, how could he have been so certain that he

was right? How could he always be so sure of his own rightness and never question himself? Never waver for a moment to see the other person's side of it? Not even for a God-given little minute? Myself, somehow, despite my young years, I always knew there was another side to everything, and that was what frightened me in this world. The other side of things, and the fact that I might not see them.

But not my brother David—oh, no. He knew all and he saw all, God help him.

I personally was acquainted with people who prayed to be like David, and likely would never make it. Was it a blessing in the end to be like him? Or was it a curse? Only God knew, I decided. All I knew was that it must be a terrible burden.

We went upstairs and David told Josie to fix supper for Mr. Cameron, to bring it down and wake him up to eat.

Without looking at me, he said. "Come and talk to me sometime when you acquire some sense."

It was worse than being slapped.

By now, Yankee officers were taking their lives in their hands to ride through the street and yell, "Women and children to the cellars! The Rebs are going to shell the town!"

So David helped me and Josie bring mattresses and pillows and blankets down to the cellar. Josie, who lived with her own mother a block away, usually went home at night, but this night David asked her to stay. He was fear-ful to let her go.

We slept in the cellar that night, all of us except David. I don't know where he slept or if he slept. He brought in extra straw from the barn to put beneath the mattresses, careful to keep it away from the hearth, warning us sternly not to put lanterns near the straw and supervising all around. Josie brought down a fresh pot of coffee and all that went with it. And soon we were comfortably en-sconced in the cellar, if that word could be correctly ap-plied to our situation, what with the constant explosion of shells going on outside.

I don't know if the correct word to describe the sound of the shells is *screaming* or *piercing* or *screeching* or *shrill-ing*, because just as they got done doing all that, they *ex-ploded* and *burst* and *violated the night* and *tore* and *ripped* and *destroyed* and *ruined* everything I felt was *secure* and *safe* and *holy* and *sacred* inside me.

I lay there under my blanket, away from everyone else, trembling. The whole world was surely breaking in two, and it would never be whole again after this night. I felt the house shaking. I pulled my blanket over my head. Everybody in the room was quiet. All that could be heard was the crackling of the fire in the hearth and the occa-sional footsteps of David upstairs.

Then some time went by. I don't know how much, because the way things were, time could no longer be measured in the same manner. The dimensions of its value now must be the number of lives lost with each shell.

I heard David's footsteps coming down the stairs. I tried not to whimper. I did not want him to think I was a sissy-boots now, along with completely having no sense.

He was walking around, likely inspecting everything. I heard him pause, checking things. Oh, I wished he'd go away. I managed not to whimper, but I knew I was still trembling. Then I was mindful that he had stopped and was standing over me.

I pretended to be sleeping.

"Tacy?" his whisper came.

I tried to breathe easily.

I felt his hand at the edge of my blanket, cautiously pulling it down from my face. I did not open my eyes. Next I felt a kiss on the side of my face, so gentle it was like a butterfly had decided to land there for just a minute, then flew away.

My heart stopped. Hearts do that sometimes. Then he adjusted the blanket so it came to just below my chin and walked away, going back up the stairs.

I stopped trembling and fell asleep.

❧

SOMETIME DURING the night, Marvelous came. She was there in the morning in a corner of the cellar, wrapped in a quilt, sitting up and grinning at me.

I had slept late in spite of everything, all the shelling, the noise, the crowds of Rebs in the street outside. Everybody else except Mr. Cameron was upstairs having breakfast. He was outside, having gone to the outhouse, accompanied there by David, Marvelous told me.

"Where did you come from?" I almost screamed it at her.

She came to kneel down beside me. "'Bout time you got up. I wanted to wake you, but that brother of yours said no, let her sleep. I came in the middle of the night. My daddy, he brought me. And David said yes, he'd keep me, and he brought me right down here. My mama, she wanted me to come. There be so many wounded in that church now, there be no place for me to sleep. And the Rebs, they're taking over the town."

"They are?"

"Yes, and my mama said, if they come into the church she'll fight them to the death, and so will the other women, before she'll go with them, but she doesn't want me in the middle of it. So she sent me here."

I hugged her. "Oh, I'm so glad you're here. Let's go upstairs for breakfast."

❧

IT WAS THE second of July, and we did not know what to expect next. The terrible shelling had stopped, yes, but only because the Confederates did seem to have taken over the town.

We were prisoners in our own village, if you wanted to think of it that way.

Outside the sky was a clear blue and the sun was bright, and I thought, eating my eggs and bacon, how any other year this time we'd be making food for a Fourth of July picnic. But I said nothing. Maybe I was finally acquiring some of that sense David had accused me of not having.

We all ate quickly, in silence.

Except for David. He had already been out and about. He told us that the Confederates had erected barricades at the end of the streets and dismantled backyard fences. "Some Rebs have been in houses, demanding to be served breakfast," he said. "If they come in here, we've got to oblige them. Tacy, you stay out of the way. Marvelous, you stay out of sight. No arguments from anybody. Give them what they want and they'll go away. We've got whiskey. Two bottles of it in Pa's study. If they ask for whiskey, give it over. And whatever you do, don't sass them."

The subject was so solemn, so unreal, that nobody said anything.

"Now, I'll be here most of the day. I've just got to escort Josie home to see if her mother came through the night all of a piece. Somebody already told me they saw our cow, Daisy, in a field near the railroad. On the way home from dropping Josie off I'm going to try to bring Daisy home, if it is her. The whole business should take me just an hour. Mama and you girls should be fine until then."

He got up, took his musket and Josie, and they went out the back door. I stood watching. He mounted his horse and helped Josie up behind him. I minded how she put her arms around his waist, hugging him close, and they were off. It wasn't far to her house, but I knew how she would lean her head against his back, how she would enjoy that ride. I wondered, *Would he?*

"It'll be all right," Mama told us. "You finish your breakfast. I'll start to clean up."

But before we finished, she was sitting down again. Turned out she had a terrible headache. "The shelling kept me awake all night," she said.

Marvelous and I brought her mattress and bedding upstairs to her bedroom and fixed things up proper-like for her, and in no time she was asleep. Then we crept down and finished cleaning up from breakfast.

Within ten minutes there was a knocking on the back door. Marvelous and I looked at each other. "Go hide," I told her.

"Likely it's my mama," she said. "She told me she might be by this morning if the shells didn't kill them all."

"No, go hide!" I insisted, as I ran to the door.

I opened it. Three Rebs stood there. Two privates and one lieutenant. "We need some breakfast, miss," the lieutenant said. "Can we come in?"

Well, you're in already, I wanted to say. Then I minded what David had told us about not sassing them. I backed off and they stood in our kitchen, holding rifles. Their uniforms were dusty, buttons hanging off, sleeves ripped, pants ragged.

"Smells good in here," one of the privates said. "I smell bacon."

"Looks good, too," the other private added. He was eyeing me.

Then they sighted Marvelous standing a little aside near the corner window in the kitchen.

The private who said he smelled bacon stepped forward. "Well, well—what we got here? This the downstairs gal?"

"All right," said the lieutenant, "take off your hats and act like gentlemen."

They did so.

"I'm Lieutenant Gregory Lewis Marshall of the Forty-fifth Georgia," he introduced himself. "This is Private Joel Walker and Private John Calhoun."

They gave half bows, as if they were at a formal dance, then sat at the kitchen table. I started to make breakfast while Marvelous poured hot coffee and got out the cream. The two privates could not keep their eyes off her.

In no time at all I had eggs, bacon, bread, cheese, butter, and jelly in front of them. They ate ravenously. I had to make three portions of eggs.

In between bites, they asked me who else lived in the house. I told them.

"My mama. She's upstairs sleeping. The shelling kept her awake all last night. My brother David. He's off trying to get back our cow. Somebody stole her."

How old was David, they wanted to know. Then, why wasn't he in the army? And where was my father?

I answered all their questions. Were there any other menfolk in the family? I said yes, two other brothers who were with the Second Pennsylvania Cavalry.

"Ho," said Private Calhoun, "they have intense hostility toward us."

"Hush," Lieutenant Marshall said. "We wouldn't be at war if they didn't. Fine group of horsemen. I've seen them in action."

Then the privates asked about Marvelous. "She bound or free?" Private Calhoun questioned. "We heard there were a lot of free darkies in this town. That some of our soldiers captured a lot of 'em and took 'em south."

"She's free." I might have said it a little too sassily.

Calhoun looked at me, his eyes narrowing. "That so."

"Yes," I said, politely now. "That's so."

"Well, then," said Private Walker, "she's up for grabs, isn't she?"

"What do you mean," I asked, *"up for grabs?"*

"What I mean," Walker explained patiently, "is that we have taken the town as of today, and you all are our prisoners. And that being the case, we can take this darkie girl here—what did you say her name was?"

"Marvelous," I told him. "Her name is Marvelous Biggs."

"Marvelous!" He near shouted it. "We can take her with us, because she is our prisoner now. Free no more, but ours. The spoils of war. And we can take her with us back down south. To slavery."

The room went silent. The coffee bubbled on the stove. I heard Marvelous draw in her breath. I looked at her briefly, then at Walker, who looked so self-satisfied, I wanted to throw a dish of eggs in his face. Then I glanced at Calhoun, who had the audacity to wink at me. If I had David's Colt .45 I would kill him on the spot, I decided. Never mind that I did not know how to use it. I would learn how to use it.

I looked at the lieutenant. He was sipping his coffee.

I kept right on looking at him. *Someone in this room had better take charge,* I thought. *And soon. Before I go plumb crazy.*

The lieutenant saw me eyeing him. I don't know what kind of look I had on my face, but he set his cup down in the saucer and smiled at me. "Great coffee," he said.

My eyes were bulging out of my head. I was waiting, and he knew it.

"Did you have something you wanted to say to me, Miss Tacy?" he asked gently.

"Lieutenant." I composed myself, though it took all the effort I had. Somehow I knew that this man would accept no less. "Lieutenant, please, sir, Marvelous is my friend. Don't let them take her away south and put her into slavery. Please, sir. She is a good person. And, she's my friend."

I wanted to say more. There was so much more I

should say! A whole war was being fought out there and people were bleeding to death, and I could not even form the words to tell it.

I have failed! I have said nothing to save Marvelous. What good am I?

The lieutenant compressed his lips, nodded his head slightly, and folded his arms across his chest. "Do you think I could have more coffee?" he asked.

I started to move.

"No." He put up a hand. "Let Marvelous get it."

Oh my God, I thought. *He's trying to tell me he sees her as nothing but a slave.*

Marvelous moved forward from her corner to fetch the coffeepot from the stove, brought it to the table, picked up the lieutenant's cup, and poured the coffee. Then she set the cup down carefully in front of him.

He looked up at her. "Thank you, darling," he said.

She nodded and moved away.

He took the sugar bowl and put two teaspoons of sugar into his cup and stirred it slowly and carefully. While stirring, he spoke. "This is a terrible war," he said, as if musing to himself. "Men are dying horrible deaths all around. And the reason, the very reason is being acted out right here in this kitchen."

He put the spoon into the saucer, poured some cream into the coffee, and considered the whole business as if the answer were in the cup. "If I could end it now, I'd end it. But I'm just an insignificant lieutenant. Nobody asks my opinion about important matters. But I'm being given the opportunity to give my opinion about an important matter now."

He looked up at his men, first one, then the other, then at me. "She's your friend," he said. "I lost two friends so far in this war. The girl stays."

I jumped up on my toes. I put my hands over my mouth so I would not scream.

"Call her over here," he said.

I did so. He gestured she should come to him. When she did, he said to her, "You are free, Marvelous. And you will stay here and stay free. You are not, and never will be, up for grabs."

Marvelous gave him a curtsy. "Thank you, sir." She ran around the table to me and we hugged.

Then Lieutenant Gregory Lewis Marshall of the Forty-fifth Georgia stood up and looked at his men. "Let's go," he ordered.

They got to their feet, looking rather shamefaced.

The lieutenant came over and extended his hand. Thinking he wanted to shake hands, I gave him mine. He bowed and kissed it. "Thank you for the excellent breakfast. We Southerners are not all savages. I don't want you to think of us all that way."

"I won't, sir."

He nodded to me, then went out.

"Oh, Marvelous," I said as we danced around the kitchen, "they're not all bad, after all. They aren't."

I don't know why it took something like this to make

me realize that perhaps they weren't. To understand that perhaps they might be people just like the rest of us, dragged into this war without wanting to be. But I did know that I would remember Lieutenant Gregory Lewis Marshall of the Forty-fifth Georgia all of my life. I never knew if he survived the war. But I always hoped he did.

CHAPTER EIGHT

MIRACULOUSLY, NONE OF this had woken Mama. Marvelous and I cleaned up the kitchen and before another hour had passed, David came riding into the backyard, leading Daisy by a rope.

Across his saddle, in front of him, he had something. Something wounded. At first glance I thought it might be a human being. At second glance, a baby calf. And then, I saw it was a dog. A wounded and frightened dog. I looked at Marvelous and she at me, and I grabbed a towel and we both ran outside.

"What do you have there?" I demanded of my brother. I never demanded things of my brother, but this time the occasion warranted it.

He slid off his horse, grabbed the towel from me, and carefully wrapped the dog in it. It was medium-size, black and white, and it was bleeding from its side. But its eyes were open and it was whimpering.

"Where's Mama?" he asked.

"She's upstairs sleeping. She's got a bad headache."

"All right. Here, you take it." He handed the poor thing over to me as if it were a bag of potatoes. And of a sudden I had the weight of it in my arms. "Take it in the kitchen. Marvelous, help her. Get an old blanket and put it on the floor. I'll be right in. Got to take care of Daisy here first. Get her in the barn and feed her. Go on, do as I say."

"Is Daisy well?"

"Middling well. Go."

Marvelous and I managed to do as he said. The dog, bless her, was docile and, beyond a little whimpering, gave us no trouble. It was Marvelous who started cleaning her wound, who pronounced it just surface deep, who didn't mind the blood, so that by the time David came in to take over, all the blood was gone, not only from the wound but from the fur.

"If women could be doctors, I'd say you should go to medical school," David told her, and I was surprised to feel jealous.

We gave the dog some warm milk with bread in it and she soon fell asleep.

Then David bade me go upstairs and get him a clean shirt, and when I came down he grabbed a towel and a bar of soap and went outside.

He may have a twisted leg, I thought, watching through the window, *but I know now why Josie is smitten with him.* She'd seen him many times like this, washing up at the pump in the yard, half naked. Often she'd made it her business to be there with him to hand him the towel. I'd thought nothing of it before. But now I did.

Now I saw why.

David lacked nothing in masculinity. He was broad

shouldered, had muscles as well formed as Joel's and Brandon's, was browned and handsome. I wondered if he carried any feelings inside him for Josie.

Then, turning, I told Marvelous to put on a pot of fresh coffee, and went outside.

"David."

"Yes, Tacy?"

"Can we keep the dog?"

He finished washing, splashed water over his face, and reached for the towel. "I suppose so, if it's all right with Mama. Not much of a dog, though."

"I think she's right nice. And I'll take care of her. Can we give her a chance?"

"Everybody deserves a chance." He reached for the clean shirt, put it on, and started buttoning. "I'm about starved. Left Josie at her mama's for a while. Got anything to eat?"

"Sure. Got fresh coffee brewing, too. The Confederates drank all the other."

"Confederates?" He stopped in his tracks to stare at me. "They were *here?* And you didn't tell me?"

"Well, I *meant* to, David. First thing. But then with the dog and all, well, other things just got in the way."

"Yeah, I guess other things got in the way," he said.

"But I'll tell you all about it, soon's we get inside," I promised.

"Yeah," he said, eyeing me steadily, "soon's we get inside."

Thank heaven, Marvelous had his breakfast all ready for him, eggs and ham and reheated biscuits, coffee, and a few other things she had managed to resurrect and make like new again. The sight and smell of it becalmed and soothed him while I told the story of what had happened.

He said not a word, just ate and listened. He chewed and drank and looked up every so often, and when he was finished, he contemplated a bit. He was scowling.

"Come here," he said solemnly.

I got up from my chair and went to stand beside him, not knowing what to expect.

"You did good," he said. He reached up, put a hand on the back of my neck, pulled me down, and kissed my forehead.

"Were you afraid?" he asked me when I sat back down.

I wanted to say no. I wanted to lie. But he would know if I was lying—he always did. "Yes," I allowed.

He picked up the coffeepot and poured himself another cup. "Good. It's good to be afraid sometimes. Did they make any unseemly advances to you? Or Marvelous? Because if they did, I'm either going to have to report them to the provost marshal's office or kill them."

"No."

He sipped coffee. "What aren't you telling me, then?"

"I've told you everything, David."

He looked at Marvelous. "No sense in asking you, is

there, sweetie? You wouldn't tell tales out of school if I threatened to hang you up by your thumbs, would you?"

Marvelous lowered her eyes. "Nosir. 'Ceptin, I don't know what it is, if it's anythin'."

He bit his lower lip. "Come on, Tacy. Or I'm going to think you're protecting them for something."

He was right. So I sighed and told him. "I liked Lieutenant Marshall," I said.

He closed his eyes for a second. "What do you mean, you *liked* him?"

"Well, because he let Marvelous stay. Because of that, of course. But not only because of that."

"Because of *what*, then? The color of his eyes?"

"If you go on like this I'm going to cry."

"If you don't go on, I'm going to give you a reason to cry."

"I think you're a crude toad! An ungrateful beast!"

He leaned back in his chair and looked at Marvelous. "We always end up like this," he told her, mildly. "We can't discuss anything but it turns into a fight."

Marvelous won't say anything, I told myself. *She knows better.* But I was wrong.

"Tacy loves you, Mr. David," she told him. And right there I wished the Rebels had taken her.

Well, that turned David around, all right. That shut his mouth for half a second at least. Now he sighed and looked at me. "All right," he said. "Let's start again. Likely I am a crude toad and an ungrateful beast. Most women seem to think so, anyway."

"Josie doesn't." I don't know what made me say that just then. I never will know what made me say that. Certainly I had the brains to know that in the mood he was in, it wasn't the right time.

"What?" He sat up straight in his chair.

I pushed mine back a little from the table, too. "I shouldn't have said that."

"Well, you said it, so explain it."

I shrugged, like it made no never mind. "I just said that Josie doesn't think you're a crude toad or an ungrateful beast. Josie likes you. And that word doesn't even cover it. I thought you knew."

He glared at me. And the word *glare* doesn't even cover how he looked at me. "Keep your nose out of my private life," he said in a grating tone. "You hear me?"

"Yes, David."

"What I do, or don't do, with any woman is not your affair. Do you hear that?"

"I hear."

"Now, to get back to your problem. Why do you like Lieutenant Marshall?"

"Because he was human. Because"—and I did not care if David would at this point understand—"he told me he lost two friends already in the war. And that he was just an insignificant lieutenant, but that if he could, he would end the war right at that moment. And because, when he left he held out his hand to me. And so I gave him mine because I thought he wanted to shake hands. But he bowed instead, and kissed my hand. And then he thanked me for the breakfast and said he hoped I would not think all Southerners were savages and he did not want me to think of them all that way. And when he told Marvelous she was free, he said she would stay here and be free forever."

David said nothing for a terrible, lonely moment.

"It just came to me, David, that I liked him. And that he was the enemy. And when it came to me that I liked him, I didn't know if it was wrong or not. And I promised myself I would ask you about it when you came home."

The kitchen was silent. We could hear the grandfather clock ticking in the hall.

"I didn't like him because he had blue eyes," I added. "It wasn't anything like that."

My brother shook his head. He put one elbow on the table and rested his head in his hand. "Why Pa ever left me in charge of you," he said, "I don't know."

I got up quickly from my chair. I bolted, started to run past him, away from him as far as I could get, but as I did he caught me by the wrist and held me firm.

He did not say he was sorry. David seldom said he was sorry. He just said, "No, Tacy, you are not wrong for liking Lieutenant Marshall. You are just ahead of all the rest of us. You have just figured out what all the rest of us are going to have to figure out how to do someday. To like each other again, after all this damned foolishness is over."

He held me like that for a few more seconds. I did not

look at him and he did not look at me. But the feelings between us could have lighted the contents of a soldier's cartridge box.

Then he squeezed my hand and I ran from the room.

CHAPTER NINE

I DON'T CARE how you dress it up, or try not to dress it up, it happened that very afternoon of July 2, shortly after our noon meal, which Marvelous and I prepared together.

Mama rescued a young Yankee soldier and saved his life.

She had come down from her nap, feeling refreshed and looking a lot better. Marvelous and I told her in the kitchen, when my brother was out of the house, about the Confederates' morning visit and how David had brought the cow and the dog home. We introduced her to Cassie and asked her if the dog could stay.

Mama looked doubtful at first, but then Cassie, as if she knew her future lay in the balance, got to her feet and hobbled over to Mama, where she sat and raised her paw. And that was all it took.

"Another schemer in the house," David said as he stood just inside the back door, watching.

"Oh, she's adorable!" Mama was completely smitten. "Of course she can stay!"

It was right after our meal, as I said, that we heard the commotion. We were still at the table when we heard sharp shouts, what sounded like orders, then in answer, a protest. And of a sudden, a yell from Mr. Cameron downstairs.

"Out of here! All of you! How dare you enter my place!"

David leapt to his feet and grabbed his musket.

"No!" Mama grabbed his arm. "No, David, I'll have no killing in my house. Let me go down and see what's going on."

"No killing? Mama, those may be Rebs down there! They specialize in killing!"

"They've been ordered not to harm the citizens, David. Especially the women and children. If a man goes down with a gun, well, that's different, wouldn't you say?"

David was stymied on two points. Mama was right, first off. And she was his mama. And when she spoke to him like that he knew better than to go up against her.

He stepped aside and let her go. Then he stood there, musket in hand, looking rather helpless. And there was no one worse to be around than my brother David looking rather helpless.

So in order to avoid appearing such-like, he ordered Marvelous to the garret, to make herself invisible, just in case they came upstairs. She went. He glared at me because he could think of nothing better to do with me for the moment. We stood in silence, listening.

"What's going on here?" we heard Mama asking.

Then came a distinct Southern voice. "Nothing to bother your head about, ma'am. This man is our prisoner.

We been followin' him for a block now, and he cut across your property and started down these cellar stairs to escape. But we're set on takin' him in. Like I said, ma'am, nothing to bother your pretty little head about."

"Well"—Mama's voice had the same tone she'd used on David only moments earlier—"my head, Sergeant, has a right to be bothered. You see, these are my cellar stairs. And this is my house. And maybe where you all come from the women don't bother their pretty little heads about such matters, but here in Gettysburg, we do. This man is wounded, sergeant. His arm is bleeding rather copiously. My husband is a doctor, away with the army. But I am familiar with such matters. And I would suggest that you leave this man with me so I can tend to his wound before he bleeds to death. And then you can come back for him later. How does that sound to you?"

There was a moment's silence. Then the sergeant spoke. "Sounds good, ma'am. We'll leave him with you. Come back for him later. Much obliged."

We heard him say, "Let's skedaddle, men," and they were gone. And David was downstairs in a wink to fetch Corporal Nelson Halpern upstairs into our kitchen.

True to her word, and with David's help, Mama cleaned, dressed, and bound his wound. She gave him some laudanum from Pa's cache of medicines and, after examining his mouth, some Aver's wild cherry pectoral for a sore throat.

Then David helped him up the stairs and into his own bedroom.

Mama prepared a tray of soup, bread and butter, and hot tea. I took it upstairs. David had Corporal Halpern sitting on the edge of his bed. David had taken off his shoes and was unbuttoning his uniform shirt.

"When do you think the Rebs will come back for me?" Halpern was asking.

"Likely they won't," David told him. "They've got bigger game to hunt out there."

"But if they do?" the young man insisted.

"They have to get past my mother first," David reminded him. "I don't envy them that. And if they do, then they have to get past me."

I set the tray on the dresser next to a basin of water and soap and washcloth David had already secured. He was about to wash Halpern, but then he saw me.

"Mama sent me up with food," I said.

He nodded and stopped unbuttoning Halpern's shirt.

The corporal looked at me. He was no older than twenty, if that. His dark hair curled around his ears. He needed a shave. His eyelashes were thick, and there was an earnest, anxious look about him that tore at one's heart.

He was nothing if not handsome.

"Take the bedspread off the bed," David directed, "then go back downstairs."

I did as he said, but I did not leave right off. At the door of the room I stopped and took one more look at Corporal Halpern. His eyes were following my every move, as though he were hypnotized.

They were blue eyes, very blue.

"What did I say, Tacy?" David asked. His voice was acid dry. He looked sternly at me.

I stuck my tongue out at him and ran from the room.

❧

THE REBS never did come back for Corporal Halpern that day. As David had said, they had bigger game to hunt out there. Because, though things had been silent most of the morning, at around four in the afternoon the war took up again, with gunshots sounding in the near distance and shells screeching in the streets.

It was after four that Josie came home. She was supposed to be home at two. She'd promised David that, and from two o'clock on he was pacing the house like a cat under a tree full of sparrows, talking about riding out to get her. The only reason he didn't was because his horse, Robin, was the last horse we owned and the Rebs would shoot David off her just to get Robin.

I was smirking to myself as I helped Mama get the makings of supper ready, not because Josie might be in danger but because David was openly showing concern for her, not bothering in the least to hide it.

Then the back door opened and she came in.

From the front hall David near ran to the kitchen. "Where have you *been?*" he demanded of her. You would think she were me, the way he demanded it. "We've been worried about you."

Josie smiled and took her bonnet off. "Well, hello to you, too, Mr. David. I'm sorry if I worried you, but I got detained because of this white band on my arm."

David scowled. "That band means you have a connection to the medical profession. Have you? Is that why you're wearing it? And carrying a basket full of bandages?"

"No." Josie set the basket down. "Dr. Dimon, my mother's friend, stopped by to ask Mama if she could put up two of his nurses for a few hours' sleep. His hospital at the hotel was hit by artillery fire yesterday, you know, and the place is filthy and disorderly. He was the one who suggested I wear the arm band and carry the bandages. Then on the way home I met so many wounded, I just *had* to stop and help them. I even went to find water to help them. That's what made me late. So don't scold me, Mr. David."

She commenced to cry then and ran from the room and upstairs.

I followed her up. As I went by my brother, I said, "Just stand there, you crude toad, you."

I found Josie in the small room she used when she sometimes stayed over. She was sitting on the bed, tears still coming down her face. I sat down next to her. "Don't cry," I soothed. "You ought to know my brother by now. He likes to hear himself yell. It gives him a sense of power. He really doesn't mean it."

She stopped crying and sniffed. "You think that's true?"

"Sure."

"Then why do you cry when he scolds you all the time?"

"I have to do something, don't I?"

She put her arm around my shoulder then. "You don't," she said. "It breaks your heart when he scolds. I know it does. I know how much you love him. And I've told him that, too."

I scowled. "You shouldn't have."

"I have a right. I'm practically family."

"Well then, I had a right to tell him what I told him about you."

Now it was her turn to scowl. "What did you tell him about me?"

"I told him that you're in love with him."

Her eyes widened. Her face flushed, then went white. "You told him *that?*"

"Uh-huh. I figured he's just too dumb to know and he ought to be told. And you'd never do it. Well, don't look so shocked. *Somebody* had to do it."

"Oh, Tacy, what did he say?"

"Got all flustered. Told me to stay out of his private life."

"How will I ever face him again? He doesn't even know I'm alive."

"Just be yourself—act like nothing's happened. It'll

give him something to think about. Maybe he'll start to act like a human being for a change."

"Oh, Tacy! I don't know whether to thank you or tell him to spank you."

I got up from the bed, leaned down, and kissed her. "Don't give him any ideas," I said. "He's got enough of his own. Now come on down and have something to eat. Mama and I made supper. As for him knowing you're alive, you don't know how worried he was when you didn't come home on time, Josie—you just don't know. Come on, let's go. I've got so much to tell you. About how Mama saved a Yankee's life today, and he's lying in David's bed in the other room, and the new dog that David brought home, and . . ."

I removed the white band from her arm and took her hand. She was giggling as we went down the stairs.

CHAPTER TEN

J OSIE INSISTED on serving supper as usual. She even chatted with us as she did so, telling us about some of the wounded she had come upon on the streets, some of the men she had helped on the way home, and how one or two had even grabbed at her skirts as she came along, begging for help.

But I noticed that she directed none of her words at David. And none of her glances. He did not pay mind to her, either. Studiously, they ignored each other.

Still, we lingered at supper. As it turned out, Mama invited Josie to sit and have coffee with us, then the two of them brought food up to Corporal Halpern and David fixed a tray to bring downstairs to Mr. Cameron. To surprise everyone, Marvelous and I did the dishes. Then I asked Mama if I could take Cassie out for a walk.

"When and if the shooting stops," she said. "And then, only on our property. And Marvelous must remain here." She was absolutely obsessed with Marvelous being kidnapped by Rebs. Especially since we had told her what had happened that morning.

It was after eight when the artillery fire finally stopped. David had gone to the barn. Marvelous, exhausted by the day's events, had taken herself to bed. I did not know where Josie was. She'd not gone home, but likely to bed herself.

I fastened a rope around Cassie's neck and took her outside. The July heat had abated and the evening had separated itself from the rest of the world. It wanted nothing to do with the killing and destruction. It was a universe unto itself, with a cool breeze, romantic shadows, and quarter moon that hung delicately overhead.

Cassie and I decided to be a part of it, and we walked out into the meadow and viewed the house and barn from a distance. I pretended there was no war, that if we went back inside Pa would be there. And Joel and Brandon would be playing a game of chess. David would be out and about, maybe down at the Globe Inn, having a drink and flirting with the girls. He used to do quite a bit of that. In the times before.

Thinking of David, I saw a light in the barn and then, at the same time, a figure going in the door.

A woman's figure. Mama, likely going to see how Daisy was.

I lingered inside the fence of the meadow awhile longer, wondering how long it would be, if ever again, that we had even a handful of horses here, wondering what had ever happened to my Ramrod. I breathed in the sweet night air and patted the head of Cassie, who stood beside me.

I don't know how much time passed before I decided to go back to the house, or what decided me when I was halfway there to go to the barn instead. But it wasn't Daisy. It was something else, some awareness of senses that David and I once had between us come to life again on this tempting July night.

Without thinking I headed straight to a side door of the barn and opened it quietly.

I got no further. I just stood there, staring, like a jackass in the rain.

Up ahead under a lantern hung on a rafter were David and Josie, kneeling in an empty stall in the hay. They were kneeling, facing each other, holding each other, kissing passionately.

Well, I supposed then that David did know she was alive and had known it for some time now.

I had to get out of there! Quick! And I had to get out of there without making a sound, or none of us would be able to look each other in the face again!

I pulled Cassie's rope enough to choke the poor thing, vowing to accomplish the task if she so much as whimpered. She didn't, thank God. The door, thank all God's angels, did not squeak. Outside, I crept carefully away from the barn for the first fifty paces, than ran as if the devil himself were chasing me.

A cloud passed over the quarter moon, and darkness enveloped me as it should have done. *I deserve such darkness,* I thought. *What am I about, spying on them?*

Think of it! David and Josie in love!

With all the killing and bloodshed going on around

us, those two scraped out a space in the hell around them and found the time and the hope to love!

I saw to it that Cassie was put to her bed for the night, kissed Mama, who was doing some knitting in the parlor, and went directly to bed. Once there, I shivered, though it was warm. I thought of them, in the hay in the barn, kissing and doing whatever else went with the act of love.

But they never even spoke at supper, I minded. *Never even glanced at each other!* And now look what they were about. My own brother David! What was it he had said to me? *"What I do or don't do with any woman is not your affair."*

It came to me then. I hadn't thought he was capable of giving such tenderness or love to a woman, of giving so much of himself over.

As I knew my brother, he never allowed himself to gamble away his feelings with anybody. My brother Joel once said, "David plays his cards close to his vest." He never exposed his feelings. Which was, it seemed to me, what love required.

It must depend on the woman, I decided, to sense what love was in a man, to bring it out of him, to dare to give of herself and to chance being hurt and turned aside. Had Josie done that? Had she taken such a risk with my brother?

I fell asleep blessing her. Over and over again.

GUNFIRE WOKE ME at four in the morning. Fierce gunfire. At the same time came a knocking at my door and my brother David's voice, melding in with what must have been cannonading.

"Tacy, get up. Now!"

Before I could answer, he came in, with no regard for my state of dress or undress. Actually I was just sitting up in bed.

"Sounds like they're fighting on Culp's Hill. Come on—bring your pillow and blanket. Come to the cellar right now."

The door closed. I got out of bed and stood there in my cotton nightgown, looking around for my wrapper. In a second, the door opened again.

"Oh, and put on some clothes. Everyone's going down. Including Corporal Halpern." The door closed again. Period, end of sentence.

I dressed quickly, then grabbed my pillow and a book I'd been reading, *Frankenstein* by Mary Shelley. I never let David see it. He wouldn't let me read it, because Jennie Wade had given it to me. I knew that. And because of the subject matter.

If he had his way I'd be reading John Locke's *An Essay Concerning Human Understanding.*

I stopped off in the kitchen and helped Josie, Marvelous, and Mama carry the makings of breakfast downstairs. I stole a sideways glance at Josie, looking to see if she'd changed any since her dalliance in the barn with my brother.

I'd read romance novels. In them the heroine always was changed after a love dalliance. Her skin tone glowed, her hair shone, her eyes glistened. Because romance with her beloved solved all her problems.

None of these improvements were apparent with Josie. She looked just as worried and hassled as the rest of us this morning. And, just as last night, she did not even glance at David, or speak to him. And he ignored her completely, too.

Is this how they were going to conduct themselves, then? Carry on in secret and in public act as if they could not abide each other?

I found myself more than a little disappointed with both of them.

WE ATE BREAKFAST slipshod-like, in the cellar, without the formality Mama insisted on upstairs, though Mama did ensure we said prayers first. She said a special prayer for the men fighting up on Culp's Hill. We knew the Culp family for whom the hill was named. They owned a farm just outside town, and their son was even now fighting for the South on the hill named for them.

By the time daylight made it possible for David to extinguish the kerosene lamps, which we'd been using for days now since the town shut off our gas supply, we'd finished our breakfast and were settling into our places in the cellar, listening to the firing from Culp's Hill.

Marvelous was sitting next to me, and between us we figured out a system by which we could tell the difference between the Confederate cannon and ours.

"Ours," she would whisper. And when a Reb cannon went off, I would return in a like whisper, "Reb!"

It seemed to go on all morning. In between playing this game I watched David and Josie. They were sitting on opposite sides of the room from each other, but every so often their eyes would find each other's and they would exchange a secret glance.

I was proud of myself for being the only one in the room to know why. I did not confide in Marvelous the fact that Josie and David were lovers. It was my secret alone.

Mama had fallen asleep again despite the gunfire. So had Mr. Cameron and Corporal Halpern, who did not look too well at all this morning.

Before long Marvelous gave up the game and dozed, too. I snuggled under my blanket with Cassie the dog, half sleepy myself. And frightened now. Because the Reb guns were getting louder and more frequent. I looked across the room at David.

"Suppose they win?" I asked him shakily. "What will happen?"

Everyone else must have been thinking the same thing. Corporal Halpern opened his eyes and looked at David, too. And so did Mama. As if my brother had some inside intelligence. As if he had the answers to it all.

He took his time responding, David did, but he considered the question carefully. Then he shook his head no. "They won't" was all he said. "We have superior firepower. And superior manpower. They just won't, that's all."

For some reason everybody took his word for it. And those who'd had their eyes closed went back to sleep. Even me.

At midmorning, two things happened to wake me.

The fighting on Culp's Hill stopped.

And there came a pounding on our front door.

David rushed upstairs to answer the door. I heard his voice and that of a woman in a brief conversation, I heard a despairing "Oh" from David, and then he invited the woman downstairs.

It was Jennie Wade's mother.

Immediately, I sat up.

"Ma." David stood at the foot of the cellar stairs. Mrs. Wade stood on the first step, a little above him.

Mama came fully awake. "Why, come in, come in." Now she stood up, shaking the sleep from herself. "Are you all right, Mary? How is your new grandson? What is he? Six days old now?"

"Ma," David said quietly, "she isn't all right. She's come to tell us, Jennie's been shot this morning. She's dead. They think she was killed by a Confederate sharp-shooter."

He said it with no emotion, David did. He seemed to be in shock. Even as Mrs. Wade was.

CHAPTER ELEVEN

W HAT HAPPENED next was that David and Mama and Mrs. Wade went upstairs, as if someone were directing them to do so, as if some angel on temporary leave from heaven was leading them with a sword and telling them what to do.

I stood at the foot of the cellar steps, watching.

At the top of the steps, the angel must have given David permission to speak to me, for he turned and said, "You stay in the cellar with the rest of them, Tacy, at least until I come back. I'll be back directly. I'm just going to escort Mama to the McClellan house on Baltimore Street."

The McClellan house was where Jennie had been shot. She and her mother had been staying there, helping her sister, Georgia, with the baby, who was only six days old.

"All right," I told David. Though I don't know if he heard me, because he didn't look as if he was hearing anything, except maybe that angel, who was likely telling him to get on with it because he, the angel, had other places to be, and *by the way, don't forget your musket, David—there are still Rebels in the streets.*

They went out the door.

The house was silent; it felt empty. I went back down the steps, where everyone in the cellar was staring at me as if I had news to tell or something.

"Stop crying, Tacy," Josie said. "It'll be all right."

"I'm not crying," I said. "And anyway, how can it be all right? She's dead. Jennie Wade is dead. It isn't all right to be dead, is it? Since when is it all right to be dead?"

She was coming toward me, Josie was, with her arms outstretched. "No, it isn't, honey, but your being hysterical isn't going to help right now. It's only going to hurt you. Come on down here with the rest of us. You can't do anything for Jennie Wade anymore."

I allowed her to take my hand. *Hysterical? Who was hysterical?* But I allowed her to take me over to my mattress where Marvelous waited for me, big-eyed, while I said things I had to say.

"I fought with her and she was my friend."

And "The last thing I did was fight with her."

And "I was supposed to wear pink at her wedding in September."

And "She never really loved Johnston Hastings Skelly. She still loved David. Did you know that? Why she agreed to wed Skelly I never knew. I think it was just to make David jealous. Well, now she can make both of them jealous, can't she?"

Josie took me by the shoulders and gently set me down on my mattress. They were all still staring at me. "I'm going upstairs to get some spirits," Josie said to no one in particular. "She needs to be becalmed. Marvelous, hold her. I'll be right down."

Marvelous held me. I cried on her shoulder. "I want David," I sobbed.

"He be right back, sure 'nuf," Marvelous promised.

Corporal Halpern came over and knelt beside me. He took out a clean handkerchief and wiped my face dry of tears. "You want some hot coffee?" he asked.

I looked into his clear blue eyes and he smiled at me. "I want to run away with you," I said. "If we leave now, before my brother gets back, nobody can catch up with us. Will you run away with me? We can go north. I know a place where we can go to get away from here. Do you want to get away from here?"

"I would love to get away with you, Tacy." He reached out and took my small cold hand in his big soft one. "And maybe someday, when all this is over, we will. But right now, if we did, your brother would be behind us with a shotgun, honey, and I want to come through all this alive. And see how beautiful you will be when you grow up."

"I'm grown up now," I told him. I knew I could scarce speak. I was trembling so. The tears were still coming.

Josie was back with something ruddy-colored in a glass. She made me drink it. "This will calm you," she promised, "at least until David comes back."

I drank it. Horrid stuff. *Why do men like spirits so?* "Maybe the angel won't let David come back," I told them all.

"What angel?" Josie asked.

"The one with the sword," I explained, "that went with them when they went out into the street."

They stayed with me—Corporal Halpern, Josie, and Marvelous. Mr. Cameron just went back to sleep as if nothing had happened. My three companions kept listening to my ravings about the angel and Jennie Wade, and eventually David did come back.

"Did the angel have to go back to heaven?" I asked him. "Or was he needed someplace else in Gettysburg?"

He immediately carried me upstairs and set me down on the couch. Mama wasn't coming home till later, he told us. She was staying with Mrs. Wade.

He looked frightened because of the state I was in, David did. So when Cassie climbed on the couch and nestled close to me, he allowed it. He asked Josie not to go home that night, but to stay. And when Corporal Nelson Halpern asked his permission not to go upstairs to his room right off but to sit next to me and keep watch, David said yes. And he said yes, too, to Marvelous, who sat on the floor beside the couch and held my hand.

When our grandfather clock struck one I heard what I identified as two Confederate cannon go off. Then came a barrage of Confederate artillery.

"We never should have come up from the cellar," I heard David say.

But none of us moved. We all just sat in our appointed places, listening, our senses deadened by now. Once again shells screeched over town. At one point David came over to the couch and reached out his arms.

"Come on—I'm taking you back downstairs."

I turned over, putting my back to him. "No, go away. I don't care if I die here!" I screamed it.

He picked me up and I held my face to his shoulder. "Put me back down," I begged.

So he did, gently. And I stayed there, covered with a light comforter while the shelling went on.

The house shook. The dishes in the cupboards shook. My bones shook. Cassie trembled and, at one point, howled. I hugged her close. Then, after about an hour and a half, it stopped, as suddenly as it had started.

Then there was a lull and we heard nothing.

David opened the front door and stepped out onto the stoop, just for a minute. He came back in. "Lotta smoke over the fields south of town," he said. "Can't see anything else. But I've got a feeling something's about to happen."

He went into Pa's study and came out with Pa's binoculars, then ran, in his peculiar limping gait, up the stairs. I heard him running that way all the way up to the garret. After about half an hour he came back down.

His face had a look on it as if he had been given a glimpse of the future.

"What is it, David?" Josie asked him. "What did you see?"

"Can't quite name it," he answered. "Maybe they will name it in the future. Maybe they never will give it a name. But when I looked through these"—and he shook the binoculars—"what I saw was not to be believed." He stopped talking for a moment and looked at each of us, one at a time, then recommenced speaking.

"Confederates," he said. "Thousands of them. All lined up in perfect formation on Seminary Ridge. Marching as if in a parade, shoulder to shoulder, across an open field that must be at least a mile across. Came right out of the woods, they did. Like toy soldiers. Marching right into federal guns. Never wavered. Just kept marching. Wave after wave of them, getting mowed down."

David put his hand over his face and paused for a moment. Then he put his hand down and looked at all of us again in disbelief. "Thousands of them," he said again in incredulity. He shook his head in amazement. "They walked right to their deaths! Right into our guns!"

None of us said anything.

"I never," David finished, "saw such brave men. Or such foolish ones. And I hope to God never to see such again."

Then he turned and walked into the kitchen. "Josie," we heard him plead, "could you please put on a pot of coffee?"

CHAPTER TWELVE

"God," David said, "has a sense of humor, you have to give Him that, anyway."

That's what my brother David said when Mama came home that evening and told us that Jennie Wade was going to be buried tomorrow on the Fourth of July.

"Don't be blasphemous, David," Mama told him sharply. "God had nothing to do with Jennie's being shot." And she would hear no more of it, not of God's part in it anyway, if indeed He did have a part in it.

It was near seven when she got home. Not dusk yet, though it seemed as if dusk had been with us all day. The dusk of something, if not the dim part of twilight. The dusk of civility, I suppose, with us this whole third day of July. We did not know what to call it.

We ate the supper Josie had made for us, in near silence. There seemed to be a quiet stillness out in the street. Mama insisted Josie sit at the table with us, and when she did, Josie and my brother scarce looked at each other. We were a sorry group. David was downcast, Mama simply worn down, Josie wary and giving David sidelong glances. Corporal Halpern was quiet, too. I picked at my food and continued to gulp back tears. Marvelous was the only normal one at the table, and she kept giving me encouraging looks to keep me going.

"You are not going to the funeral tomorrow," Mama said quietly to me.

"I have to go," I said.

"You are not," Mama said firmly. She could be worse than David when she wanted to be.

My voice quavered. "But I never got a chance to say goodbye."

"None of us did," David reminded me. "Now bide what Mama says. No arguments." His voice was low but firm.

After supper there came a knock on the front door, and when David answered, a Reb soldier stood there, bedraggled, humble, and gloomy.

He looked at the musket in David's hand, which had the barrel pointed to the floor, then at all of us, who stood a distance behind David, and took off his hat. He had a head full of yellow curls. "Sir," he said. "I'm from South Carolina. I don't wanna fight no more. I don't wanna be a soldier no more. Sir, all'st I want is some civilian clothes an' to run off. Please, sir, could you all give me some civilian clothes?"

David paused for a moment before answering.

"Sir," the soldier went on, "I saw Pickett's Charge this afternoon. All those godforsaken soldiers marchin' across Seminary Ridge into those Union cannon. I can't, I just can't, sir, be part of an army that does such to its men."

I saw my brother nod his head. Heard him say, "Come on in."

His name was Rucker, Private Allen Rucker. His family owned a plantation right outside Charleston, he told us. "My two brothers are officers, but I would not go to war at first. My pa was one of the leaders who made the pledge that if a Republican was elected president, the state would leave the Union. Because I wouldn't go for a soldier, Pa near threw me off the place. So I went and joined up as a lowly private. I didn't want to be made an officer because of his influence."

"But what will happen to you now if you run away?" David asked. "You can't go home to your pa's plantation."

Mama had rustled up some civilian clothes for him and was feeding him at the kitchen table.

Allen Rucker just looked at us. "You all gonna win the war," he said. "I could see that today. There won't be a plantation left to go home to."

He left a short while later. He would not stay awhile to rest, as Mama had asked him to. Rebs were trickling back into town, he pointed out to us. Didn't we see? He showed us, out our own front windows. Sure enough, he was right. We saw stray soldiers in tattered gray, not prancing about confident and overbearing as they'd been in the last two days, shouting orders, but almost slinking, muskets at the ready, ducking into doorways or forcing open cellar doors.

Mama fixed Allen Rucker a cloth bag of vittles and David gave him some Yankee greenbacks and directed him a safe way out of town, and he left. I stood at the back door, watching him go. For some reason I started to cry again, and David came over to lead me back to the couch.

"What have you got for her, Ma?" he asked.

Whatever she "had for me" she gave me with a cup of tea, and David sat over me while I drank it. The last thing I remember was him saying, "So they've already got a name for it, have they? They're calling it 'Pickett's Charge.'"

Next thing I knew he was carrying me upstairs to bed and taking off my shoes. I awoke the next morning in all my clothes.

❧

FIRST THING I heard through my open window was somebody in the street yelling.

"Move, move, hurry up, we are retreating!"

I jumped out of bed. From my window I saw Confederate soldiers running up the street, hurrying toward the Diamond, the central square in town. A Rebel officer on a horse was yelling at them. "Let's get the hell out of here, before we're captured. Can't you see the damned Yanks?"

There was a lot of confusion and cussing and shouting.

The courthouse clock chimed six. As I ran downstairs, my mind felt like a picture puzzle, and I shook it to put the pieces into place.

Today is the Fourth of July.

Jennie Wade was killed yesterday.

Her funeral is today and Mama is not going to let me go.

By the time I reached the kitchen I had a reasonable scene of events before me, and I hoped I did not look as confused as I felt.

They were all dressed and at the table for breakfast already—Mama, David, and Marvelous. Even Corporal Halpern. Josie was serving coffee. All looked up as I entered the room.

"Tacy, how are you?" Mama asked.

"I'm tolerable," I told her. "I heard the soldiers in the street say they were retreating." I slipped into my chair. "Is it over? Is it all over?"

"Just about," David answered. "But we can't run about the streets just yet. There are still Reb snipers about."

Well then, I wondered, *if it is over, if we won, why is he so solemn? What is it he isn't telling me? Is there more? Something terrible more I don't know about?*

"What time do we go to the funeral?"

"*We* go at nine o'clock," Mama answered. "You aren't going. You are staying here."

"But I told you, Mama, I'm tolerable fine."

"You aren't going! I'm still in charge around here and that's that!" David's voice was as stern as it ever had been to me.

I bit my bottom lip and looked down at my plate. "You mean I have to stay here alone while you all go?" I felt tears coming. His rough voice could always do that to me.

"No," he said. "I'm staying with you."

Mama gasped. "You're not *going,* David?" She could not believe it.

"No." He would not look at her.

Josie stared at him now.

He would not look at her, either. And then it came to me then. He was in a foul mood this morning. Not even the Yankee victory over the Rebs here in our town could cheer him out of it. Why?

Josie and I exchanged a secret glance across the table.

Nobody said much of anything through the rest of breakfast. Afterward I saw Mama go over to David as he stood looking out the window in the parlor.

She touched his shoulder. "Darling," she said.

He turned his head toward her. "I'm sorry, Mama. I didn't mean to be rude."

"It isn't that. I worry for you. I think it would be better for you if you go."

"I can't, Mama. I can't bring myself to go."

I was drying dishes and Josie was washing, her back to this scene. Marvelous was wiping off the table. Only I was privy to what was going on. And listening when I shouldn't be.

I turned away from them then, but I still heard Mama say, "All right. I'll make your excuses. But do this for me. Be kind to Tacy, will you?"

"She needs discipline," he said. "Why can't she just obey without making a fuss?"

"Not today," Mama said. "Not today, David."

He said something, real low. I don't know what it was, but it sounded like some kind of a promise.

CHAPTER THIRTEEN

THE FIRST THING David said when Pa had told him he was in charge of me, responsible for me when Pa left for the war, was "I don't know if I can do it, Ma. I don't think I can do it."

I heard him say it. I was listening when I shouldn't have been, like I always do.

"Of course you can, dear," Mama told him.

"But what if something happens to her? I'd be responsible. You know how Pa cherishes her. His only girl. The youngest. The baby. I'd have to answer to him."

"What could happen to her, David? You're being silly now."

"You know how capricious she is. Always running about and getting into things she isn't supposed to be getting into. She never listens to you. I tell you, Ma, she's spoiled. You and Pa and the boys and I—yes, even I—spoiled her. And now I have to take over. It isn't fair."

"You'll just have to be firm, David. Set boundaries. She adores you; you know that."

He'd groaned then. And ever since he worried that something was going to happen to me. And he'd have to answer to Pa. I told myself that's why he was so mean.

That, and because it ate at him that he was not able to go for a soldier. I told myself that all the time.

❦

SOON AS WE finished the dishes, David had to take Josie home to fetch some black clothing for the funeral and to check on her mother. They were quick about it, and when they returned she asked me to come upstairs and help her do up her hair.

She always wore her hair the same way, Josie did, and so I knew there was something amiss. The only reason she was attending the funeral in the first place was because she'd offered to help out with the refreshments afterward.

David hadn't wanted her to go. They'd had quick, quiet words about it before he'd agreed to take her home, but she was going anyway. I was glad to see him give in, glad to realize that he could not always get his way with her. That no matter how much she loved him, and I know the boundaries of her love went far, that she would not let him dominate her. *She is good for him,* I thought. He needed that.

Upstairs, I found that she needed more than help with her hair. She needed, desperately, to talk.

"We scarce spoke a word all the way to my house and home again," she told me. "And it wasn't anger on his part because I'm going to the funeral. It had nothing to do with that." She was fussing with her hair. Now she stopped, dropped her hands to her sides, and looked at me.

"Oh, Tacy, he still *loves* her. He still loves Jennie Wade!"

"She's dead," I reminded her.

"But it's all come back to him, how much he loves her. And I don't think he loves me anymore, if he ever did!"

I did the only thing I could do. I put my arms around her. "He loves you, Josie," I told her. "He's just being moody right now. It'll pass. David is nothing if not moody. And you are the only one I've ever met who can pull him out of it."

She looked me in the eyes. "May I confide in you, Tacy?"

"Of course."

"You won't ever let on to him that I told you?"

"I promise. As you can see, David and I don't get on the way we used to anymore."

"He had best love me, Tacy. Oh dear Lord, he had best love me. I've given myself to him. Do you know what I mean?"

I told her yes, I knew what she meant. And I told her then that if David had given himself to her in that way it surely meant that he loved her. Because my brother David seldom gave of himself, with his feelings, to anyone, ever, if at all. And as for the heartfelt love, the physical love, I doubted whether he had ever bestowed it upon any other woman at all.

She quieted down then. "Do you really think I haven't lost him, then?" she asked. "Do you really think that he'll come back to me?"

I did not know, for I did not know if I would ever get my old brother David back again, either. I seriously doubted it. But I lied and said yes.

❧

AFTER MAMA and Josie left for the funeral, Marvelous wanted to go to the church to see her mother, and so David said he would take her. He was torn between allowing me to stay home with Corporal Halpern, who was intent on going back to his unit as soon as David returned, and taking me with him and Marvelous.

"I want to stay with Corporal Halpern and say goodbye," I told him. "We've become friends."

David was not about to give me anything I wanted this morning, despite any promise he made to Mama about being nice to me.

"You come with me," he said. He said it right in front of Halpern. I don't know where my brother got his boldness sometimes. I know he liked Halpern, too.

"I'm staying," I told him firmly.

It was chancy. He raised his eyebrows at me. "You going to mouth me now?"

"Yes."

He sighed, wearily. "You want to spend the day in your room?"

We were in a deadlock, which Halpern broke.

"I promise, sir," he said quietly, "I'll be on my honor with Tacy. I think too much of her. And you, to act otherwise."

The "sir" business gave David a turn. Nelson Halpern was scarce two years younger than David.

Taken aback, David said all right, I could stay. He knew Nelson had his musket, in case any runaway Reb wandered in. And so he left with Marvelous.

When they were gone, I got some paper and pencil and invited Corporal Halpern to sit with me on the couch. "The first thing is, we exchange addresses," I told him. And so we did. I took the name of his unit, and then I ran upstairs and found a likeness of myself. My brother Joel had sketched it and it was true to life. It was in a locket.

"I've been keeping this, hoping to give it to someone someday," I told him shyly.

"You sure you want to give it to me? Maybe there's someone else you should be saving it for."

Because he had made the promise to my brother to be honorable and I knew he would not break it if a hundred Rebs were at the door, I kissed his cheek when I gave him the locket. "I'd rather give it to you than anybody else in the world," I said.

He'd just shaved this morning. His face was smooth and soft. So were his lips when he turned to kiss me.

I never forgot Nelson Halpern. He was the first young man who ever kissed me.

WHEN DAVID returned I was fixing up a parcel of food for Nelson even as Mama would do, and wrapping it in a brown cloth. Then he and David said goodbye out on the front steps and he was gone.

It was awkward when my brother came back. The courthouse clock struck eleven, and he just stood there for a while out on the front steps. I heard music from a distance, saw our troops ushering some ragged Confederates out of town at bayonet point. I opened the front door behind David and saw dead soldiers in the street, theirs and ours. Dead horses, too. And people coming out, up and down the street, to sweep and wash off their front steps. From a distance I could see wagons rumbling into town, likely farmers bringing in food, eggs and milk and such.

Food. I knew then what to say to David. "Do you want lunch?" I said to his back.

"Too early for lunch."

"Well, I'm about starved. And I'm going to make lunch. You can eat or not. It's up to you."

I started back to the kitchen when he turned. "Tacy?"

"What?"

"You're being damned mouthy to me this morning."

Oh, God. "Do you want bacon or ham with your eggs? We have both."

"Did you hear what I said, Tacy?"

"I'll make both."

The coffee was done. I'd made it earlier, given a cup to Nelson before he left. David came over to the stove just as I was pouring a cup. "What in hell is wrong with you, Tacy?"

I handed him the cup of coffee and he took it. Across it our eyes met. "Same thing's wrong with you. I'm crying inside over Jennie. Just like you are. And outside over Nelson. Same's you are over Josie. Only I'm not afraid to admit it."

"I ought to smack your behind for that."

I shrugged, picked up the bowl of egg mixture, and poured it into the fry pan. "You wanna slice the bread or do I have to do that, too? Last time I cut my finger. It bled pretty bad."

He took the bread board, knife, and bread over to the table and began to slice.

I minded the omelet. "I'm afraid I'm never going to see Nelson again," I told him. "I'm afraid he's going to get killed in the war. And I liked him lots."

"If Meade pursues Lee today instead of letting him get away, the war could soon be over," he said.

He sat down at the table with his coffee. "How much is lots?"

"I don't know. How much is it supposed to be?" I fetched two plates, filled them with omelet, bacon, some ham, and set them on the table.

He commenced eating quietly for a moment.

"You asking me?" he said. "You asking *me* about love? Is that what you're doing?"

I looked down at my plate. "I figure you must know."

"Oh you do, do you?"

I nodded, but I did not look at him. "How can you be sure when love is real?" I asked. "And when it isn't?"

He took his sweet time about answering. "When it makes you miserable," he said quietly, "that's when it's real. When it makes you want to die one minute and live forever the next. When"—and here he paused to take a sip of coffee, put his cup down, and looked right at me— "when you would do anything in the world for this person. Follow this person into hell and you don't care who knows it. That's when it's real."

He bit his bottom lip. He scowled. He was somewhere else now, not here with me. And he was angry.

And then he was here with me, again. He looked up at me across the table. "What did she say to you before I took her home this morning?"

"Who?"

"You know damn well who. Josie. When she asked you to go upstairs with her and help her with her hair. Josie never needs help with her hair. What did she say?"

"I can't tell, David. I promised."

"The hell you promised. Anyway, you owe your loyalty to me. I'm your brother. I'm the one who takes care of you. Who would fight to the death for your honor if I had to. Tell me, *what did she say?*"

"You told me not to interfere with you and any woman, David."

"Tell me!"

I hadn't really promised. Josie hadn't asked me to. "She was afraid you didn't love her. That you were still in love with Jennie. She asked me if I thought that you would come back to loving her again."

"And what did you say?"

"Oh, David!"

"Tell me."

"I told her yes, you would."

He scowled at me so that I wanted to duck under the table. He contemplated the whole business for a minute, worrying it to the bone. And then the frown vanished and he said in a low, kind voice. "Would you get me some more coffee, sister, please?"

CHAPTER FOURTEEN

THEY BURIED Jennie Wade in the garden behind her sister's house.

"Can't get near a cemetery," Mama said when she came home, "and with all the plots needed now, well, they're worth gold."

Anyway, Mama went on, out of a desire to fill the silence, I suppose, that Jennie belonged there, with the flowers in the backyard. Nobody said anything, except Josie. She said she thought she might set herself to baking, that other women at the funeral had told her they were going home to do the same thing.

"I think I'll just whip up some biscuits and gruel to bring over to Christ Lutheran, if it's all right with you, Mrs. Stryker," she said.

"It's fine with me," Mama told her, "but it'd be even more fine if you started calling me Nancy."

Josie looked startled. "Oh, I couldn't do that, ma'am," she said.

Mama sighed sadly. "I do so long sometimes to hear my name. With my husband away so much, there's no one in the house to say it."

Mama was so clever. Josie smiled. "All right, then, Nancy. I'm going to make some biscuits and gruel, real quick-like, and bring it over to the church."

"Better be quick-like," David put in. "It's fixin' to rain soon. Tacy, why don't you help her."

❧

Because there was still some rifle fire being exchanged in town, David took Josie and her supply of food over to the church the back way. I didn't offer to go with them, for I wanted to give them this chance alone. I told them it was already starting to rain and I had to walk Cassie, which indeed I did. They had to make a couple of trips back and forth with the food and I thought, *Good, it will do them good. Better yet if they get wet together.*

It was when they were making their second walk over and I was lingering with Cassie in the backyard, getting somewhat wet myself, that I heard the thunder.

At least I thought it was thunder. And in a way it was.

The thunder of horses' hooves, coming down our street in front of our house.

There were breastworks a bit up from our house, set there by the Confederates, for what reason I did not know, and I doubt if they knew either. For by now it had become clear to me that the Confederates' reasons had been vague about most everything they did. What happened, I think, is that this bunch of horses had escaped of a sudden from somewhere, and now found themselves free, and decided to run down our street.

Then they came upon the Confederates' breastworks and halted for a second, likely thinking *What in the name of all that is holy is this? Have the Rebs no sense at all? Do they think this can stop us?*

So, after thinking about it half a second, they did what came naturally, which was to go around the breastworks, which meant going through the nearest open front door of a house and passing right through it, one at a time, right onto the wooden back porch, and off it into the backyard, which they found very pleasing.

Now this house was about three houses away from ours. And the woman who owned it, Mrs. Netherwood, happened to be sweeping off the back porch at the time and just stepped aside quickly enough to avoid being trampled to death.

We heard later that she threw away her broom, raised up her arms, flew aside, and yelled, "Oh, Lord, what will come next?" Which ought to give a body an idea of what kind of a state the citizens of Gettysburg were in at this juncture.

Anyway, there I was, three houses down in our yard with Cassie, who was already in a state of apoplexy. So I ran her into the house and came out again to see what was going to take place next.

There were about six horses. And they had found the grass in Mrs. Netherwood's backyard more than pleasing.

They found it downright delectable. All but one horse, who had lifted up its head and was sniffing the rainy air in my direction. And then walking slowly and sniffing toward me.

Ramrod!

My own Ramrod!

No, I told myself, *it can't be,* even as she kept walking through the yards, coming to me. *This does not happen in real life,* I told myself. *Stolen horses do not come home again. That happens only in happily-ever-after books where the frogs turn into princes and the cruel stepmother gets what is coming to her. Never in real life.*

Finally she was on the other side of our fence, leaning her head over to me. I hugged her. She nuzzled me and whinnied, and I cried and went out the gate and led her inside. Oh, she was in grievous shape, ragged-looking and unbrushed.

She had no saddle on. I led her right to the barn, where I gave her water, brushed and fed her, and stayed with her for the rest of the afternoon. I talked to her like I used to. Outside the dark was coming on and it was pouring rain.

In what seemed like a little while, the barn door opened and someone came in with a lantern and a blanket. I didn't look to see who it was.

"You could have at least let Mama know what you were about. She's been frantic worrying about you."

I was inside Ramrod's stall, leaning against her neck, soaking wet.

He put the blanket around me, then fetched a horse blanket, came inside the stall, and put it around Ramrod. "So she's come back, eh?"

"If you scold and ruin all this for me, I'm never going to speak to you again in my whole entire life."

He patted Ramrod, ran his hands over her flanks. David knew horses. "She's all right. She's in good shape. You should leave her to sleep now. And come on into the house."

He touched my shoulder, then my hair. "Come on," he said gently. "I'm glad she's home. Glad for you."

I went with him.

"It's been some Fourth of July, eh?" he said.

❧

It was raining all the next day, the fifth, and I couldn't go outside, so I cooked some more with Josie. And besides the biscuits this time, we got together crocks of apple jelly, pickles, preserves, bread, and chicken. We raided Mama's pantry in the cellar, with her permission, of course.

They wouldn't have let me go outside, anyway. David had been out early to help the U.S. Sanitary Commission, which had already started to arrive, clean up the streets. "There's dead heaped all over the streets," he told us when he came in for breakfast.

Mama wouldn't let him in the house until he washed up thoroughly at the pump outside.

He sat at the table, his hair still wet. "The Sanitary Commission is going to spread chloride of lime on the streets. I think that may be worse for us than the germs from the dead. They say we may have to keep our windows closed in the middle of the day."

"In this heat?" Mama was horrified.

"It's either that or invite the germs in," David said.

"I saw a man go by before," I offered, "with a wagon-load of cut-off arms and legs."

"Tacy!" Mama scolded.

David glowered at me. "Leave it to you to say the wrong thing at the right time.

"There is a stench outside," he continued. "The next time I go out to help, I'll be wearing a mask, and I can get you all some bottles of pennyroyal and peppermint oil from the Sanitary Commission to ward off the smell."

"You're a darling boy, David," Mama told him. "I don't know what we'd do without you. Be grateful you have your brother, Tacy," she told me, "and don't sass him so. You don't know how lucky you are to have him."

"Oh, Ma," David said, embarrassed. But he glowed at her praise and looked at me smugly.

I stuck my tongue out at him across the table and Mama saw it.

"Shame on you, Tacy! Do you know how many girls have brothers who will never come home from the war? Now go and give him a kiss, right now!"

Oh, God, there was no going against Mama when she took on like this. I got out of my chair and went around the table to David. I hesitated only a moment. In that moment David's and my eyes met. I couldn't tell what his said. But I leaned over to give him a quick kiss on the cheek.

Surprisingly, he reached out and put his arms around me and held me for a moment, his face against mine, then let me go.

It rained all the rest of that day and I couldn't go out, not even to walk Cassie or visit Ramrod. David was out helping the Sanitary Commission, whose members had increased on the streets, when Sam, Jennie Wade's brother, came over. Mama didn't want him to work so soon after his sister's death, but he said he wanted to. So he did things around the place that needed doing. And I began to change my opinion about him, for he looked solemn, as I'd never seen him before. And I began to wonder how it felt to lose a sibling.

I knew he loved Jennie.

In front of the courthouse the Eighth Pennsylvania band played patriotic songs all day in the rain. The sound of the music was muffled and wandered like something trying to find its way home, halfhearted and knowing it did not yet belong in this atmosphere, but telling us, *There is still room for music in this world, there is—just listen and give us a chance.*

Sam told us, when Mama invited him in for something to eat, that wagons were already coming into town with food and medical supplies from Maryland and New Jersey and other parts of Pennsylvania. "Somebody from the Sanitary Commission told me that soon's they heard a few days ago that there was a battle here, they started packin' up their wagons," he said.

I helped Mama cook some food for Mr. Cameron, who was pestering David to take him home. Mama didn't want to let him go home to an empty house and insisted David go inside with him and make sure everything was all right. I thought of his son and wondered if he'd ever come home again. And David threatened to hang me up by my thumbs if I ever mentioned a word of his son to Mr. Cameron.

It stopped raining for about an hour after supper, and David walked him home.

So we were alone again, except for Josie, who stayed, because now that her mother could finally get out of her house, she went to see her sister in Hanover.

❧

I KNEW BY the end of the day that something was gnawing at Mama's innards. And I knew what it was.

After supper I cornered David when I found him alone in Pa's study, having a drink of whiskey, all alone. He was sitting moodily at Pa's desk.

"David?"

"Yes, Tacy. Aren't you in bed yet? Why would you want to drag out this forlorn day?"

"Ma's spirit is all over the floor."

"I'm aware of that."

"Do you know why?"

"I'm having thoughts about it."

"She's brooding over Pa. And Joel and Brandon. She's wondering why, when the fight is over, they haven't come home."

"Has she told you that?"

"No."

"Then how do you know it?"

"I just know it, David."

"I forgot. You have special powers."

"I don't think you should be mean to me now."

"No, I shouldn't. I'm sorry. I've had a bad day. Picked up and helped haul off too many mangled bodies. Not a task to make you want to dance about." He gave a deep sigh. "Well, with all the wounded, I suspect Pa's still tied up somewhere. Same with Joel and Brandon. Likely Old Crankcase won't give them leave."

"Who?"

"Colonel Richard Butler Price, their commanding officer. There's a lot to do out there yet, even though the fighting's over. If anything had happened to them, we'd have heard. Same goes for Pa."

I nodded my head.

He took a sip of his drink, set the glass down, and looked at me then, really looked at me for the first time. "You're scared," he said, "aren't you?"

I did not answer.

"You don't believe a word I've just said."

"Yes, I do."

"You're a damned bad liar. You ought to learn to do better than that if you're going to lie so much."

He was hurting, I could tell. And he was scared, too. Scared that something had happened to Brandon or Joel.

"They could at least have sent home a message, couldn't they?" I asked him. My voice wasn't working so good anymore. "Even Pa. He could have."

"Oh, stop it," he said angrily. "Yes, they all could have sent home messages. But they didn't. Why? I don't know why. Because they didn't have paper or pencil. Or because they meant to and didn't. Or because they live in a different world than us at the moment. Who knows? You can scold them all when they get home, Tacy. But they'll be home. I promise." Then he put his arms on the desk, crossed them, and put his head down on top of them. And spoke no more.

I went around the desk and put my arm on his shoulders and kissed the top of his head. "Thank you, David," I said.

He grunted. Then said, "Go to bed. It's late."

I went. Cassie went with me. She slept with me now, Cassie did.

CHAPTER FIFTEEN

I WAS ALONE in the house for a couple of hours on the morning of the seventh. It was Tuesday. David was helping the Sanitary Commission to move their things to their new headquarters in the center of town, on the corner of Baltimore and Middle streets. It was the old Fahnestock Brothers store.

Josie and Mama had gone over to Christ Lutheran with more food and stayed to help with the wounded. I was safe with Cassie. She was turning out to be a first-rate watchdog.

It was almost eleven in the morning when she started barking and growling and going toward the back door, even before the knock sounded.

I was not supposed to let anybody in.

But I peeked through the kitchen window.

A Yankee officer stood there. His fine-looking horse was tethered to the railing of the back porch. I saw the Springfield rifle in the sling that hung from its saddle, and for a moment something clicked in my head, but no, I thought, no. And then I minded, what harm could a Yankee officer do? I raised the window sash. "Yes?" I asked.

"Tacy? Don't you recognize me? You going to let me in or not?"

Brandon! My own brother Brandon! Come home as sure as God made railroad ties.

I pulled down the window sash and ran to open the door.

At that moment, Sam came to take his horse to the barn. Brandon turned to say hello and to give Sam directions about his horse's care. But just for a second. Then he turned to me and for a moment he stood, in his blue cavalry uniform, face browned, eyes sparkling, grinning down at me. He took off his hat, reached out his arms, and hugged me, lifted me right off the ground in a bearlike embrace.

"Oh, Brandon, you're home!"

"Sure am."

I thought he was never going to release me, but finally he put me back down on my feet.

"Where's Ma? Is Pa home? Where is everybody? Got any coffee on the stove? That dog going to bite me?"

I quieted Cassie, who obeyed. I answered his questions and introduced Cassie, who sat and offered her paw, proper-like. I led him inside, took his hat, jacket, gloves, and sword. I held my hand out for his pistol, but he shook his head no.

He wanted a cold glass of water. I fetched some and he drank it down in one gulp, then wiped his mouth with the back of his hand and stood there gazing around as if he'd never seen the place before.

I thought I saw tears fill his eyes.

"I'll get coffee," I said softly, for I minded that I was interrupting a flow of memories.

He grinned down at me. "Place looks good. I dream of it at night. Got anything to eat?"

"Sit down. We've got plenty to eat."

I turned to fetch the coffee, but he grabbed my wrist, gently, held me back, and looked at me. Really looked at me, his blue eyes going over me, seeing everything. "You're growing up," he said, as if I'd done something behind his back. "I don't know if I like that. Can I still sit you on my lap?" He put a hand on top of my head, took a swatch of my hair and ran his hand down it to the end, where it touched my shoulders. "Getting prettier, too. But girls will do that, won't they?"

I blushed and said nothing.

"God, I'll wager you're giving David a run for his money."

I smiled.

"He treating you all right?"

"Yes."

His eyes narrowed and he put his other hand under my chin. "Heard there was hell to pay in this town. Heard about Jennie Wade, too. Darn shame. She was a nice girl. Pretty, too. How's David taking it?"

I shrugged.

His eyes narrowed and he released me and sat at the table. I fetched him a cup of hot coffee and he sipped it gratefully. "You're not telling me things, sister mine," he said jokingly. "All right, there's time. When I get home, we'll have a nice talk and you can tell me things. We'll catch up. I just got a couple of hours and thought I'd come home and let Ma know we're all right, me and Joel—we've come through it all fine. All the hell out there. And believe me, it was hell."

I prepared some food, half breakfast and half lunch, and we talked.

I told him all about Josie and David. He listened intently. "So old David finally found himself a love, did he? Good for him. As I recollect, Josie is a pretty little thing. David does like them pretty, doesn't he?"

I wanted to ask him about his lady love. Before the war, he'd been seeing a girl named Emily Sedgwick from Hanover Junction. But I made no mention of her now, for I did not know the status of their relationship. Was it over? I did not want to ask, for if it was, I did not want to cause him pain.

All I knew was that when it became obvious that the Rebs were coming, her parents had taken her and gone to relatives in Philadelphia.

But now he brought forth her name.

We'd been silent for a moment, so I knew he was contemplating something special. I'd learned from dealing with David when to keep a still tongue in my head.

Then he spoke, quietly. "Have any of you heard anything about Emily's family?"

"No, Brandon. But some of the people who left town are starting to come back. The Zieglers have returned. So have the Thorns and the Tysons. And the McCrearys. I'm sure they'll be back soon. David said he heard their house wasn't damaged at all."

He smiled. "You're a sweetheart for not bringing up her name," he told me. "You're very considerate. We're corresponding, although with the war it's been difficult for letters to get through. I'm telling you, but no one else yet. We're still courting."

"Oh, good. I like her, Brandon."

And no, he hadn't seen or heard of Pa, either. "But don't worry," he said. "Anything bad and you would have heard. One thing you'll soon learn in life, Tacy, is that people love to pass on bad news fast. Good news they have no interest in."

Then he told me that in a few days the army was going to set up a prisoner-of-war camp in a barn on the southwest corner of Baltimore and High streets.

"At least four hundred Confederate soldiers," he said. "And guess who's got the honor of guarding them? Colonel R. B. Price's Second Pennsylvania Cavalry. We're commissioned to guard the field, all the prisoners, wounded or not, and stragglers, with one hundred infantrymen to assist us."

I stared at him. "You'll be near home then, Brandon. Mama will be so happy."

"Yeah. That's one good thing about it," he said.

He left shortly afterward. "If Ma was home my visit would be longer," he explained, "but now I'm going over to the church to see her."

He went upstairs to his old room, to look around, I supposed. He came down with some books for himself and Joel. Then he went to the barn for his horse.

When he came back I had some cookies and biscuits and slices of ham and cheese wrapped up for him and Joel.

He put on his sword and coat and hat, hugged and kissed me. I went outside with him.

He mounted his horse. "Orders," he said, "from your commanding officer: Don't grow up too much more. Not yet. I may still want to sit you on my lap."

His horse was anxious to go, but he held the reins taut. He made a fine figure, looking down at me steadily, as if he wanted to imprint something on his brain. And then he winked at me, raised his hat, and was gone.

I stood there alone, feeling as if some spark had gone out of my life. I'd forgotten how wonderful life could be with my eldest brother, Brandon, around, how he always made everything all right. We never argued, never fought. To do such would be unthinkable.

If I did something that displeased him, he'd say something in a kindly, joking way, and you didn't realize until after he had said it that he'd admonished you in such a way that you were bleeding inside where your heart was supposed to be.

And it wasn't because he had hurt you; it was because you had hurt him by whatever you had done. And all you wanted was to be forgiven.

But now he was gone and the world had turned cold on this hot July day. And it was as if he had never come.

CHAPTER SIXTEEN

IT SEEMED THAT by that afternoon there were more people in town than ever before. The *Adams Sentinel,* which had started publishing again and which Mama brought home with her, said the town had twenty-one thousand wounded from both sides and not enough surgeons or nurses or volunteers.

"All kinds of people are coming into town to help," Mama said, "by wagon, by rail, any which way they can. All kinds of people. Not to mention the relatives of the wounded. And there's no lodging for them."

She stood there in the kitchen, sipping coffee I had ready for her. I also had a chicken roasting in the oven. It was the least I could do. She was exhausted but happy. She'd seen Brandon.

"Oh, he looked wonderful," she'd told David, glowing. "Oh, I thank God he and Joel are alive!"

Now she'd made a decision and she wanted advice about it. "David, what do you think about us giving lodging to some needy people? There are people coming to town who have no place to stay."

"No," David said without even thinking about it.

"But David," she protested. "We have such a lovely home!"

"Ma." He was weary, too. He'd been volunteering all day with the Sanitary Commission. Now he was delivering supplies to the army field hospital and, at the same time, casting an eye out for Pa. He still hadn't come across him.

"Ma," he said, "I may be asked to bring a wounded case into our house. I'd rather do that if it's all the same with you. And anyway, we don't know what all is going to happen in the next few days, do we? Let's wait and see."

"All right," Mama agreed. She always minded what David said.

❦

WHAT DID HAPPEN later that day was that Marvelous came back to us. Her mama had gone home for a spell, she told us. Just for a spell, to see if the house they'd been living in was still standing. It was the tenant house on the Crawford Farm, but a battle had taken place on the site and the house had been used as a Confederate aid station.

"My daddy gettin' together a whole lotta men," Marvelous told us proudly, "an' with his two-horse team an' wagon he been hired to bring coffins to the battleground where the dead bodies be. He can haul nine filled coffins at a time. Mr. Warren, he only gots a one-horse team. An' he can haul only six coffins at a time!"

"Marvelous!" Mama was horrified. "Don't speak of such things now. We're glad to have you back, child, but little girls should not speak of such matters."

David, who had fetched Marvelous from the church, disagreed. "Ma," he told her, "there are no little girls left in Gettysburg anymore."

Within less than an hour, Pa came home.

MARVELOUS AND I had been sent to bed. I had two single beds in my room, and when she stayed with us Marvelous slept in the other one.

She was already sleeping, but I was not, when Pa came in. I heard his voice, jumped out of bed immediately, put on my robe, and ran downstairs.

He stood in the hall, kissing Mama, his valise on the floor next to him. I stood on the bottom step, hushing Cassie, who sat trembling next to me.

I waited while they embraced. Then David shook hands and answered some questions, and Pa hugged Josie and looked around. "Where's my little girl?" he asked.

I ran to him, into his arms. Mama had taken his coat and I nuzzled my face close to his shirtfront. Seeing this, Cassie came wriggling over on her stomach, wagging her tail.

I started to cry on Pa's shirt front, unashamed of my

tears. "Oh, Pa." It was all I could say. What else was there to say? And then, of a sudden, I could not stop crying.

"Come on, Tacy—what kind of a welcome is that?" David was saying in the background.

But Pa did not care. He took me by the arm over to the couch in the parlor, sat down, and held me in his lap, close to him, and let me cry. He kissed my forehead, wiped away my tears, and then finally I *was* ashamed of myself. I sat up and smiled at him.

"I don't mean to be such a baby, Pa," I said. "I'm not a baby anymore. Really, I'm not." I slipped off his lap and clung to his hand for a moment.

He smiled up at me and I saw wrinkles around his eyes that I'd never taken mind of before. Lines around his mouth. *He looks like Brandon will look someday,* I told myself. *Yes. Why did I never notice before how much Brandon resembles him?*

"You can always be my baby, Tacy," he said. Then he took the drink David offered him, sipped it slowly, and began to tell us where he'd been for the last few days.

"On Culp's Hill," he said. And for some reason he did not look at us when he said it. He looked instead into the glass of amber liquid, as if that was the only place he could bear to look while speaking of what he had to tell us.

"Before that I was in a field hospital a little outside town, near a battlefield. A hospital made of tents, near some barns. I worked there during the battle. Then, after it was over, I heard a rumor that my boys had fought on Culp's Hill. I suspected it was false, but I had to go and see for myself. I thought, suppose they were and they're wounded? I was so tired by then that anything seemed possible."

He paused, took a sip of the drink, and went on. "So I went up there. Well, once you entered the woods, you right off got feelings of gloom and felt that you should turn around and go back, because if you didn't, you'd never be the same.

"But I went on. First thing I saw was a corpse, and next to it a torn and bloody pocket Bible. Everywhere I looked there were torn-apart bodies, and personal belongings. Letters, photos, shoes, blankets, haversacks with their contents spilled about. Bodies piled up all over the place.

"And the people who were not dead were walking around looking for relatives, looking like ghosts themselves in the mists. There were some soldiers who'd been sent up there to bury the dead. But they had to identify them first. Then dig the grave and leave a marker telling who they were."

Pa fell silent, shaking his head. "I stayed and helped them. For two days. In my haversack there, I have, in my *Physician's Handbook,* the names of those we buried and the location. We buried many of them by the breastwork built by the Twelfth Corps. But then I took sick. The sun was so hot and I had naught to eat, and I figured I'd best come home before they had to bury *me.*"

He set his empty glass down and rubbed his eyes.

"Come to the table," Mama said softly. "Josie's got some good food. Then you should go to bed. You need rest. You're exhausted, Brandon."

David helped him in to the kitchen. I was allowed to stay up and sit quietly at the table, too. But there, mostly we talked of things that had happened at home in his absence. He devoured his food. And then David helped him up the stairs and into bed.

Pa slept past noon the next day. And when he woke he was still weak and what Mama called only middling well. He wrote a note, which David delivered on horseback to the field hospital where he worked.

❦

David returned with a note from a Dr. Robert Schell, who was a lieutenant colonel and head of the tent hospital, saying that Pa was suffering from extreme exhaustion and ordering him to stay in bed for at least a week.

Pa slept, on and off, for most of the week. When he wasn't sleeping, he was talking about going back, about how they needed him.

John Will, proprietor of the Globe Inn, came to call. Pa had once brought his son John through a fearful bout of pneumonia.

We sat and listened while John Will told Pa how people were being arrested for collecting lead bullets and unexploded shells from the battlefields. "Young boys," he said, "have learned that ammunition manufacturers are paying thirteen cents a pound for lead bullets, and so they're on the fields scavenging."

"It's so hot," he told us, "that the provost marshal issued an order prohibiting the exhuming of graves on the field. People!" And he looked at me and David. "Do you believe that people are already coming to dig up the graves of soldiers just buried?"

"I'd believe anything," David said.

"Well, no more, son. It's against the law now!"

By the middle of the week Pa came down with a fever. He did not want to eat, so Mama tried feeding him special foods, and she sent me about town with David to try to find the makings of it. To special places like Dr. Robert Horner's house, which was a mini-depot, where relief goods went for the Second Corps hospital. Dr. Horner had worked with Pa at the tent hospital outside town. When he heard of Pa's illness he sent around a note inviting us to go to his house on Baltimore Street Hill for beef tea and wine. So we went there, and to the confectioner's store for the sugar and lemons Mama needed for her special recipes.

By the end of the week Pa was in delirium, and David took another trip to the field tent hospital for a remedy from Dr. Schell.

While David was gone, Pa was raving about the dead

on Culp's Hill and how he needed to get back there to help bury them. And put the names in his book.

In his ravings he was talking to David. "We've got to go, David," he said. "I can do it, if you'll help me. You'll help me, won't you, David? Won't you?"

He was saying such when David came into his and Mama's room with the medicine.

"What does he want me to do?" David asked Mama. She'd been sitting there the whole time, holding Pa's hand, and when she wasn't doing that, setting cold cloths on his brow.

"Nothing," she told David. "Nothing to worry about. Just help me get this medicine in his mouth and settle him down."

I left the room as they did so. I waited out in the hall for David to come out.

CHAPTER SEVENTEEN

Whrn David came into the hall and saw me there waiting, he gestured with his head that I should follow him downstairs. And when I did, he asked me in the parlor, "What does Pa want me to do, Tacy?"

"I'll tell you," I said, "if you'll make me a promise."

"Don't play games with me, Tacy. This isn't the time for games."

I had done some quick thinking while waiting out in the hall upstairs for my brother to come out of Mama and Pa's room. And I knew what I wanted. Furthermore, I knew I had half a chance of getting it from David, who was, at this moment, glaring at me.

"Tell me right now what Pa wants from me."

I wanted to do for Pa. I saw no reason why David and I could not go up to Culp's Hill and do the job that he had been doing. David could bury the bodies and I could make note of them in Pa's *Physician's Handbook*.

Why not? It would help Pa, make him feel better, and it would help us.

Somewhere along the way I had decided that while Pa was suffering from fever and delirium, all along David and I were suffering from a disease, too, only there was no medicine for it.

We were both suffering from guilt. About Jennie. And about having done nothing for the war effort. Hadn't David been just about killing himself these last few days trying to make up for not going for a soldier? And I? What had I done? Marvelous had done more.

"Tacy!"

"What?"

"Tell me what Pa wants from me. Now. No more shilly-shallying."

His tone brooked no argument. After a tone like this, David took action.

"He wants to go up to Culp's Hill to bury the dead. And he wants you to go along and help him."

David scowled, thinking, and nodded his head. "When?"

"Now. Soon as possible."

More scowling. "He can't go. Be a long time before he can do anything that strenuous."

"I know, David."

"What else did he say? Anything else?"

I nodded, inventing my lie as I went along, thinking that this was all too good to be true. "He said that it would take two to do the burying job, you and him. And one more to record the name and location of burial in his *Physician's Handbook.* And that should be me."

Now he *really* scowled.

"You!"

"Yes, David, that's what he said. Me. He said I could be trusted to write the names in his book. That he didn't want anybody outside the family writing in it. You know how he feels about that book, David."

He nodded slowly. "Never even let any of us read it. You ever read it?"

"No, David. I don't think Mama ever did, either."

He grunted and did more thinking. "Surprised he'd allow you to go along and see all those horrors he spoke of up there. Well . . ." He scratched his chin. He had a day's worth of beard. "I'm going to have to think this over a bit. Right now I'm hungry and Josie's making supper. Come on, let's eat. Get Marvelous."

"What about Mama?"

"Doctor said that remedy would put Pa right to sleep. I expect she'll be down in a minute. Don't say a word about this to her, you hear? Or to Marvelous or Josie."

Not even Josie? That meant he was serious about it. "Yes, David, I hear."

❧

PA DID SLEEP and we had a quiet supper. I was especially on my good behavior, so as to be agreeable to David. After supper I offered to clean up and do the dishes with Marvelous so he and Josie could take a walk outside. It was such a beautiful evening.

David gave me a peculiar, surprised look and said "thanks," and they went out.

Before they came back I fetched a book for Marvelous, my old copy of *Fairy Tales* by Hans Christian Andersen. Marvelous could not read as well as she should for her age. I was helping her and she loved fairy tales. While she was involved with the book, I crept upstairs. Mama was in her sewing room. Pa was sleeping.

I secured his *Physician's Handbook* and left the room with it. I seldom did important things behind Mama's back, but I understood that if David and I went to Culp's Hill I'd have to go without telling Mama.

I knew that she would not approve. Oh, maybe she'd allow David to go, begrudgingly, only because when push came to shove David was a man and she could not hold him back. But never me. So I'd have to sneak off. And make it up to her later.

Downstairs I hid Pa's book behind a pillow of the couch, where I sat waiting until David came home.

❧

FORTUNATELY, AS IT turned out, Mama was so taken with Pa, with worrying about him and tending him, that she scarce paid mind to me in the next day or so.

As a matter of fact, everything fell into place for me so perfectly that I began to become worried. It was as if my life were charmed. And I knew better than that. My life was never charmed.

Marvelous went back to the church to help her mother the next morning. After she left, David told me that yes, he was going today, and yes, I could come along provided I obeyed him in everything he said and gave him no mouth about anything. He would leave a note for Mama.

"Don't say anything to her," he ordered quietly. "We don't want to worry her. When we come home all in one piece tonight, she'll see it'll be all right to let us go back tomorrow."

So David was, in his own way, conspiring against Mama, too.

But he still had to get around Josie.

We were leaving at ten o'clock on this sixteenth day of July. He told Josie about nine o'clock, and she fixed some food and water for us to take in our haversacks.

At nine thirty, I could not find David, but I heard some murmurings behind the almost closed door of Pa's study. Now, I am not one to ignore murmurings behind an almost closed door, so I listened and sneaked a glance in, too.

David was holding Josie close. "I don't want you along," he was saying. "It's going to be downright stinking up there."

"But you're taking your little sister."

"She wants to go. She wants to do it for Pa. I can't say no to her at this point. I've given her so much crap lately. I've got to make it all up to her somehow."

"You've got things to make up to me, too, David."

He kissed her, then. He told her he loved her. And that if she would have him, he wanted to marry her.

He said it all soft and dear-like, my own mean-mouthed brother David. And she said yes. And then he said that he had to be off and he would see her tonight. I ran, light-footed as I could in the stupid rubber-soled boots I had to wear, right into the parlor, where I waited for him, scowling.

"You're late," I scolded him. "Where have you been?"

"I told you: no mouth," he said.

And so we were off to a good start.

CHAPTER EIGHTEEN

WE RODE OUR horses as far as Evergreen Cemetery, and there we tethered them under a tree near the archway. David gave a guard a two-dollar bill to guard them, and we started to walk to Culp's Hill.

First we had to walk past McKnight's Hill. It was really just a knoll, but it was there that we saw our first corpse, lying facedown near a small spring. His hands were reaching out, clutching small tufts of grass. His haversack and canteen lay beside him.

David knelt down and turned him over. "Maine," he said. "He'd been trying to fill up his canteen. His musket is gone."

We looked around. Within a short distance were a lot of other Rebs and Yankees. David stood up. "Let's go," he said.

We went on. A short distance, still on McKnight's Hill, we saw a Confederate body cut in half, lying there in grass, which was red with blood for about two yards all around it. I wanted to stop, but David grabbed my arm and pulled me forward.

Then we climbed the wooded sections around Culp's

Hill and the bright sun overhead dimmed, as if we were walking into a fairy story. Only this was instead like walking into the part of it that was owned by the wicked witch who was preparing poisons to kill the prince and princess.

First we came upon body parts.

Legs and arms, as if to introduce us to what was coming. As if to prepare us for the rest.

David walked in front of me, bade me follow directly behind and halt when he did. He stopped once, just to look up.

"Look at the trees," he told me. He spoke in a whisper, and I gazed up.

All around us the trees were still standing, mute evidence of what had happened here. They were standing, yes, but you could see where the minié balls had shot away the bark and made holes in the trunks.

Some had no bark left. They were, most of them, as mangled and torn as the bodies that lay on the ground all around them. Only it was their destiny to live on if they could and remember the hell that had gone on here. And if not, if they could not bear it, then they must die.

The trees had given of themselves, too.

"Oh, it's terrible, David," I moaned.

"Yes." That was all he said. Then he went over to one particularly beautiful oak into which an iron ramrod was fastened, jammed in far. He set down his things and tried to pull it out. But it would not come out. So he cursed and tried some more, but it would not budge. So he bit his bottom lip and gave up. He picked up his things and we went on.

We headed for the place Pa had told us about, the breastworks built by the Twelfth Corps, but we became disoriented and couldn't find it. Then we smelled coffee and the aroma drew us in the direction of some soldiers from the Third Wisconsin, who were already burying some dead. There were six of them and they waved at us.

We went over to them and David shook hands and introduced his "little sister" and told them what we were about and how we were here to continue Pa's work, how Pa was a doctor with the Union army, and they directed us to the breastworks.

They offered us some coffee, which they'd been brewing on a small fire. We took out our cups. I offered them some sugar cookies Josie had sent along. She'd sent more than enough. We visited about ten minutes, then went on our way to find the breastworks.

Once there we found the graves that Pa had dug and marked and recorded in his book. We opened and read the book together, figured out Pa's system and where I should write the names of those we buried that afternoon.

In the next three hours or so, we had to decide which of the many bodies that lay about to bury.

The one that was legless, with the flies buzzing about what was left of it? And if so, mustn't David first find the legs and bury them with it? He made me step back, then searched the pockets of the man's jacket, where he found what he was looking for. A letter with his name on it.

"Write this down in Pa's book," he directed. Then from the ground where he was kneeling next to the body, he looked up at me. "Are you all right?"

I said yes, that I was, though truth to tell I was a little dazed. I did not know a body had so much blood in it. And I had never seen a man with no legs before. It did not seem to bother David, and I would certainly never let him know that it disturbed me.

He gave me the man's name and I wrote carefully: *Corporal Albert Sydney Sawyer of the 20th Connecticut.* I also wrote where he was buried: *On Culp's Hill, by the 12th Corps breastworks.*

"There are some legs over yonder," I told my brother.

"Got to dig the grave first." He took up his shovel and commenced to dig, thanking the Lord for the rain and the soft ground and remembering how Pa had told him it had to be deep. In no time at all he had a respectable grave, had retrieved the legs and had them placed in the hole with the soldier. Having covered it all over, he took out of a sack some light wood he'd brought along to make grave markers. While he was going for the next body I was the one who wrote, with a lead pencil, the name and regiment of the dead man on the marker.

"They'll designate someone to come and carve it on later," he told me. "No time to do it now."

The next soldier was Private William Sensebaugh, also

from the Twentieth Connecticut. He'd been shot in the chest and his right arm was in tatters. Just as quickly, David dug the grave and buried him, made the grave marker, and while I went about my business writing his name on it, and again in Pa's book, David went to choose another body.

Only before he did this, he ran his hand across his forehead and planted the end of his shovel in the ground. "We haven't eaten anything yet," he reminded me. "You hungry?"

I nodded yes.

"Why didn't you say something? Come on—let's go over to this clump of trees, away from the dead."

I followed him to the trees, where there were some rocks, and we took out our food and ate. If you faced away from the battlefield, looked out over the hills toward town, you could pretend you were on a picnic and not on a gory mission. You could make believe there were no dead around you.

We sat in silence. "It's really beautiful up here," David said. "Gotta bring Josie up here someday when all this mess is over."

He grinned at me and I gave a small smile back. "Sorry you came?" he asked.

I shook my head no.

He finished the rest of his food and wiped his mouth. "Damned war," he murmured. "Ruined everything for everybody. And now I hear that Meade didn't pursue Lee, but let him get away across the river. So it'll go on for a couple of more years. Lincoln's gotta get himself a better general than that. Well"—he stood up and stretched— "let's get back to work. The afternoon is almost gone."

We went back to work.

All in all we buried three more bodies. Then the man came.

I didn't know what time it was. The sun was low in the west, though, so it must have been about six o'clock already. I was worn down, and if somebody hadn't come I think David would have gone on working until dark. He's like that, David is. Once he's involved in something he just keeps right on going, never wants to quit.

We didn't hear the man coming, and he was on a horse, too. We didn't hear the horse's footfalls.

All of a sudden he was just there. I looked up and saw him first. A dumpy-looking man wearing a canvas coat. I recollect wondering why he was wearing a canvas coat in the July heat. And he was carrying a gun, too. A rifle.

First thing that came to me was that David did not have a gun. He hadn't thought it necessary to take it along to a cemetery. He'd had so much else to carry.

I worried about that for half a second. David always carried a gun.

"David," I said.

He was busy digging a grave and didn't hear me at first, so I said it again. "David."

"What?" He was annoyed at the interruption.

"Somebody's here."

He stopped digging. He took off his hat, shoved his

hair back, and looked up at the man. "Can I help you?" he asked. "You lost?"

"Don't think so," the man said. He was from the North, didn't have a Southern accent. He slipped off his horse but kept his rifle. He offered his hand to David. "Name's Daniel Sensebaugh, down from Connecticut earlier this day."

David took off his glove and shook hands.

Sensebaugh. I must be overtired, I thought, *but why does that name ring a bell?*

"Is this the site of the breastworks of the Twelfth Corps?" he asked.

"You've got it," David told him.

"Well," Mr. Sensebaugh announced, "like I said, I come down earlier today by rail with my mother to get the body of my brother who was killed the other day on this here hill."

Oh. Sensebaugh. We had just buried him.

"I'm sorry about that," David said.

"Yeah, well so am I. And my mother. I've put her up at the Globe Inn. I've got a coffin all ready to take my brother home in. Tomorrow. Guess I'll have to look around and find him." He gazed around the hill at all the bodies. "God Awmighty, what a slaughter. Well, there's a couple of hours of light left yet for me to look." He started to walk away.

David did not look at me. He bit his lower lip and looked down at his boots for a minute. But just for a minute. Then he turned and called out. "Mr. Sensebaugh!"

The man turned. "Yes?"

"Don't bother looking. Your brother's here."

"Where?"

David pointed with the shovel. "Here. We just buried him. That's what we're doing here. Burying the dead and marking their graves and keeping an account of where they're buried for future reference. My sister and I. We've been working at it for hours. Others are doing it also. At different places."

The man walked back to us. On his face was a look of pleasant surprise. "Well then, you've saved me a lot of trouble, son. Now you can just help dig him up and put him on my horse and I can take him back down the hill into town."

David stood there, straight and tall and firm. "No sir," he said quietly. "I'm afraid I can't do that."

"Well, why in hell not, boy?"

"Why, you see, sir," David said softly, "it would be against the law. The provost marshal gave orders that no bodies are to be exhumed. By anybody. Not even family members who come from afar. No sir, I'm sorry. I can't do it. And I can't allow you to do it, either."

CHAPTER NINETEEN

<hr/>

THE MAN JUST stared at David for a moment as if my brother was speaking a foreign language. Then, when Mr. Sensebaugh spoke again, he spoke as if he were addressing a five-year-old child.

"Now, look here, son, let me say it again. All's I came for is my brother's body. It'd take just a minute to dig it up. Dig it up, son. Not exhume it. I'm not one for fancy language. Up in Connecticut we don't use fancy language. You just buried him. When? How long ago now?"

"Within the last couple hours," David said.

The man nodded gravely. "Couple hours," he repeated. "So now we just push the dirt away. It isn't even settled yet. And we take him out. A simple matter. No need to attach a legal term to it. Or cite any provost marshal's order. Just let me have him and I'll be on my way."

"Can't do it," David said again.

"For God's *sake,* son, the provost marshal doesn't even know my brother's been buried!"

"My name's David. David Stryker. And *I* know he's been buried."

Mr. Sensebaugh was quickly getting aggravated. He took a deep breath, reached into an inside coat pocket, and drew out some paper money. "Good Yankee dollars." He held them out to David. "It's been my experience in life that almost everybody can be bought off. Now come on. You people in Gettysburg have taken a beating, I hear. Suffered a lot of damages. This ought to help some." He held out the money.

David stood rigid. "I can't be bought," he said quietly.

Sensebaugh frowned. "You're a damned fool," he said.

David just shrugged.

"Now I'm through fooling around, Stryker. Enough's enough. It's getting late. I've come a long way and I'm tired. My ma's waiting. She's all torn apart. I can't let her down. Now if you don't want to dig him up, step aside, give me the shovel, and I will. Or you'll suffer the consequences."

With that, he shifted the rifle in his arm.

Still, David did not move. "You'd best get on your way, Mr. Sensebaugh. I've made up my mind about this."

"And so have I," Sensebaugh said. He drew up his rifle, aiming it at David. "I'm not wasting any more time."

But I knew my brother David. He had made up his mind, too. It was like before, like the decision he'd made when he'd ripped up the note Mr. Cameron's son had left for his father in our basement. I knew that note was just as important a decision to him as the digging up of this body here and now.

And the decision just as crucial. And instant. No wavering. Just black and white, right and wrong. And no gun would put him off.

I heard the click of Mr. Sensebaugh's rifle and I screamed, "David, no, give him what he wants."

"See? Your little sister has more brains. Give me what I want."

David waved me back. "Be quiet, Tacy. And stay away." He turned and gave me a small smile. Behind him in the west, the sun was setting, and he was backlit against it. I could see in just half a second a sort of peace in his eyes, a sense that he knew at long last, what he was about. "It's all right, Tacy, it's all right," he said.

"One last chance," Sensebaugh was saying at the same time.

Then David's "No, I said. I can't. I won't."

And then the shot. So loud in the quiet woods, echoing over the dead, the last shot of the war on Culp's Hill, the shot that welcomed my brother David to their ranks, where he had always wanted to be with them, alive, and hadn't been allowed to. But was allowed now. Because he had come to them late, but he was here now, doing his part and darned if he wasn't going to do that part to the last of his ability. Darned if he wasn't going to give, as they had, to his last full measure.

I screamed. Mr. Sensebaugh's horse neighed wildly and reared, turned, and started to run. And he after it.

I ran to David, who had collapsed on the ground.

The sun disappeared behind the mountains, leaving only a winking glow and some red. But its red was as nothing to the red of David's blood.

CHAPTER TWENTY

HE WAS LYING still when I got to him, his eyes looking up at me, and he was bleeding from his chest. All kinds of thoughts whirled around in my head.

Has he been shot in the heart? If so he'll die instantly.

Maybe not, there is blood all over his shirt. He could be shot elsewhere.

What can I do? Stanch the blood. Or try to. I know that much. I'm a doctor's daughter, after all. But with what? And then what? Suppose I can't stop the flow? And how can I get him out of here? There is no one about.

All this went through my mind in the half a second before I knelt down beside him.

And then I did not what I knew as a doctor's daughter, but what I knew as the reader of romance novels. I lifted up my skirt and tore at my petticoat. I ripped it savagely, tearing it until I had a sufficient amount of cloth to apply to David's wound and absorb the blood. I held it there firmly.

"Good girl," David said weakly.

"I'm wearing more than one petticoat," I told him. "Do you hurt a lot?"

"I'll be all right," he lied, "but I could use some water."

"Well, you hold your hands over the cloth for a minute and I'll fetch the water."

He did so and I got the canteens, two of them, and lifted his head and held one to his lips.

"I wish someone was about," I said.

"Someone will come soon," he assured me.

He sounded like Mama now, calm and hopeful. It worried me. And it was dusk, which worried me more. "Do we have a lantern?" I asked.

"I brought one, yes."

"God, David, you're wonderful."

"Don't flatter me. It'll make me believe you think I'm dying."

"You're *not* dying, David. I won't let you die."

"What are you going to do about it?"

"Just you shut up about it, is all."

"You going to mouth me now? Is that what you're going to do?"

Tears came to my eyes. "Yes. You can't do anything about it, so I'm going to mouth you."

I saw tears come into his eyes, but all he said was "It'll be coming on to dark soon, won't it?"

"I suppose."

"Go over there and get the lantern. And some matches out of my haversack. Go on. Can't sit around here in the dark."

I fetched the lantern and lighted it. The glow of it was comforting. David was still bleeding and growing weaker. Sometimes he closed his eyes for a few moments, "just to rest," he told me.

I was growing more frightened, and then I saw the moon rising and the first star in the heavens.

"What will happen," he said quietly, without opening his eyes, "is that Ma will be frantic with worry by now. And if Pa is sleeping, she'll wake him, if she hasn't already. He'll send someone up here to look for us. When they come, don't forget to tell them we have horses down there. Pa knows just where we are, Tacy. You don't have to be frightened. They'll find you."

I stared hard down at him. "Me? What are you talking about?"

He took my hand. His own hand was cold. "I'll be gone soon, Tacy—you might as well accept that. I haven't long now."

"David."

"Hush, please." His voice was weaker now. "I've things to say. A person knows when he is dying. Now listen to me, please. What I did with that man who shot me I'm not sorry for. I did the right thing. You tell the authorities all about him, hear?"

"Yes, David."

"What I am sorry for is the way I've treated you."

He started to cough. Half coughing and half choking. I lifted his head. Some blood was coming out of his mouth. I grabbed a piece of my petticoat that I'd set aside and wiped the blood away. I gave him some water.

"Don't talk, David."

"No mouth," he said, and went on. "I've been mean to you, Tacy."

"It's all right."

"Isn't!" The word was forceful. "Not right! I'm sorry! Wanted you to know!"

He fell silent, breathing heavily.

Then he spoke again. "I love you, Tacy. Always did. You're my—" More coughing, more blood from his mouth.

Again I wiped it away.

"Baby sister."

"I know, David."

"Means a lot to me. Always did. Just couldn't seem to"—more coughing—"keep you in line when Pa left. You forgive me?"

"Yes, David." I leaned down and kissed the side of his face. It was feverish.

He nodded his head and gestured with it to the west. "Light over there," he said. "Somebody coming. See? Told you."

I looked. There was no light. "I see, David," I said. There were tears in my voice now.

"You tell, you tell Josie that I love her, you hear?"

"I'll tell her," I promised.

"You tell Ma the same. But tell Josie I love her."

"Yes, David." Tears were coming down my face

now and I did not try to stop them. I did not wipe them away.

"Be careful lighting that lantern again when it goes out."

I nodded my head. I could not manage, anymore, to answer.

He lay back. I released my hand from behind his neck. He breathed with difficulty for a minute or two while he grasped my hand and smiled at me.

He said, softly, "You be good. No mouth."

And stopped breathing. Then, he was gone.

I felt him go. A wind came up of a sudden from nowhere, where there had been no hint of a wind before. It blew through the wounded trees around me and they lifted their leaves as if in respect. It whirled around for about five minutes, like a serious storm was coming, but there were no clouds in the sky.

I knew it was lifting David's spirit to heaven. I felt him going.

I sat there while the currents of air did what they must do, while they vibrated in circles, making me giddy, then quieted down and let the night close in.

The lantern had gone out and I felt around for the matches, found them, and, as my brother had told me, was careful lighting the lantern again. *How had he known the lantern would go out?*

I will not pretend that I was not afraid for the next hour or so, alone there by the graves of those we had buried, with the other dead lying all around me on Culp's

Hill, and my brother David, dead right next to me. Oh, how I wished I had asked to bring Cassie along! Would someone never come?

I drew my knees up under my skirt and rested my head on them, drew my arms around my head, and shivered. I waited. I don't know how long. It was not cold, except in my heart.

And inside me my emotions were warring for dominance, both terror and sorrow.

I do not know which won that night. By the time I saw the lantern light come up the hill in the distance and the two riders on horseback, I think that it was a draw. But I no longer cared.

CHAPTER TWENTY-ONE

Two MEN approached on horseback, and at first I was scared. Then I saw they were Brandon and Joel, both in uniform.

"Tacy!"

They were near on top of me before I knew it, scrambling down from their mounts.

I struggled to get to my feet, then realized I had David's head in my lap. When had I taken his head in my lap? I raised my arms to them.

Brandon stood over me, Joel just behind him. Both their faces showed horror, no less.

"My God," Brandon said. He knelt on one knee and put his hand on the side of my face. "You all right, honey?"

I could not speak, but my tears, quiet tears, started down my face again.

"How long has he been dead?" Joel asked. He came to kneel on the other side of me and set the lantern down beside him. Gently, he took David's head from my lap and set it on the ground.

I looked at his dear face and spoke, "I don't know how long it's been. Since dark came."

Joel was going to be a doctor, like Pa. He'd just started medical school when the war came. Now he opened David's shirt in the lantern light and looked at him. "Shot right near the heart," he said.

He took his gloves off, put his arms around me, and hugged me strong. Then he drew back, looked me in the face, taking my measure. He felt my forehead. "Your eyes are all swollen from crying," he said. "Otherwise you look all right. Likely all you need is a powder. We'll let Pa decide. Are you all right? Hurt anywhere?"

I said I was all right.

"You tell us what all happened here later, sweetheart," he said. "We have to get you home now. Right, Brandon?"

"Right," Brandon said. "You take David. I'll bring Tacy."

With few words but lots of understanding, they worked together. You could tell they were accustomed to working together. Brandon fetched his blanket roll and Joel's and tossed them to his brother, who wrapped David in them expertly. Then Joel carried him on his shoulder over to his horse, where he secured him.

It was as if he'd done this all before.

Brandon picked up the haversacks and put the canteens in them, and I put in Pa's *Physician's Handbook*.

"Anything else?" Brandon asked.

"The shovel and the lantern," I said.

"Leave them. We can come back."

"Our horses."

He looked around. "Where?"

I told him. "We can't leave them. Please."

He agreed. Then he lifted me in his arms and put me on his horse so I'd be behind him on the way down the hill. He instructed me to hold on tight. We found our horses where we'd left them and the same guard still there.

The guard looked at Brandon and then at the body of David thrown over Joel's horse. "I heard a shot," he said. "I saw the man ride away like all hell was after him." He shook his head. Then, out of his pocket he drew the two-dollar bill that David had given him.

He gave it to Brandon. "Give it to the little girl," he said. He gestured at David's body. "He gave it to me. Don't want it. Anybody needs me to testify I will. Saw his face, the one who did the shooting, when he came in here and when he went tearing out, I did. Know what he looks like."

Brandon thanked him and we went on our way.

I wanted to ride Ramrod home, but Brandon said no. "You're not strong enough," he said. "You just hold on tight to me."

So he tethered Ramrod to his own horse and David's horse to Joel's.

I gave him no mouth.

CHAPTER TWENTY-TWO

I SHIVERED AND cried on the way home, unable to believe what all had happened. I leaned my head on Brandon's back. Joel was ahead of us, and I could hear Ramrod's hoofbeats and her snorting behind. I clung to my brother because he was the only real thing in the world right now.

"What are we going to tell Mama and Josie and Pa?" I sobbed out at one point.

"Don't worry about it," he said. "Joel and I will handle it."

"It's my fault, all my fault. I encouraged him to go up there and finish Pa's work."

"I don't want to hear that out of you *ever* again, Tacy."

Brandon's voice was as stern and severe as it had ever been with me. It stunned me into silence. I'd forgotten he was a captain in the cavalry and could summon forth a voice like that. But I did not know how to respond. And when I did not, he asked, more softly, "Did you hear me?"

"Yes, Brandon." I hiccupped. "I hear."

He reached a hand down and touched mine where it

held his waist. He said nothing, but for a moment he covered my hand with his own, gently, and we went on in silence. I was crying more now, silently, and was glad he could not see.

In time we were home. The boys went right to the barn, as if they had discussed things ahead of time. Brandon lifted me down from the horse and told me to stand right where I was. It was soon apparent to me that they did have a plan.

Joel untied David's body from his horse and set it on the floor. Then they took off the horses' tack and put the horses in the stalls. They fed and watered them, as if we had all night. I just stood and stared. Then, the tasks done, they looked at each other.

"Pa's surgery?" Joel asked.

Brandon nodded. "That'd be best. You got keys?"

"Always have 'em."

Brandon nodded again. "Don't disturb him too much. The authorities will want to see . . ." His voice trailed off.

"I understand. You going to tell them?"

"No. We'll all do it together. I'll wait for you. But we have a problem first."

"What?"

"Tacy here. Look at her. She's full of blood. All over her dress. We go in with her looking like this and Ma will faint dead away before we open our mouths."

Joel took off his hat and scratched his head. "Yeah." He mused a bit. "Only one thing to do. You two come in the surgery with me. You take her up the back stairs, while I'm laying David out, and get her changed. Then come back down, quiet-like, and we'll go in together."

It was agreed upon. I looked down at myself. I hadn't realized it, but the front of my dress was full of blood. David's blood. I started to shake all over again, seeing it.

Their plan worked fine. I supposed their plans always did. Brandon and I heard voices in the parlor—Pa's and Mama's and Josie's—as we crept up the back stairs from Pa's surgery. That was good. We wouldn't run into them upstairs.

I'd taken off my shoes and Brandon, his boots.

His cavalry boots went up over his knees. He carried them now. In my room he set them down on the floor, then went right to work.

"Take off the dress," he said.

I just stared at him.

"Oh, come on," he said. "Dammit, I bathed you when you were a baby."

"I'm not a baby anymore."

"Yeah, I know—you're all grown up." We were whispering, and he came over and unbuttoned the back of my dress and pulled it over my head. I stood there in my petticoat, the one I hadn't had to rip up, and my chemise, which showed the tops of my new bosoms. I was always so proud of them, yet now I was embarrassed. But Brandon paid no mind.

He went to my closet and pulled out a dress, a blue one. "Put this on."

I slipped it over my head. It, too, buttoned in back. He did the buttons for me.

"All right, let's get out of here and get this over with."

We crept back downstairs to Pa's surgery, where he put on his boots and I my shoes. Then we went out of there and around the house to the back door, the three of us. And, for some strange reason, maybe because we did not want to just walk in on them and announce out of the blue, *Here we are, we're back—and, oh yes, by the way, David is dead,* because of that, we knocked.

❦

THE NEXT DAY or so is a blur to me. I recollect that I fainted once. I do not recollect at what juncture it was. It could have been anytime between when we went in that back door and started telling Mama and Pa what had happened and the time we came back from David's funeral at the cemetery of Christ Lutheran Church.

But somehow now that it comes back to me I distinctly remember that it was before the funeral. It was when I was standing there between Brandon and Joel, telling Mama and Pa the whole story of how David had come to be shot. Josie had been put to bed with laudanum, in shock already. Pa had asked question after question of me, until we got to this. And it was then, when I was telling him what David had done to provoke the shooting, that I felt myself getting wobbly.

"Because he wouldn't dig up the body? That's why

the man shot him?" Only Pa didn't say *man*. He said a cuss word.

I leaned against Brandon for support. It was all flashing in front of me again. "Yes, sir," I said. And I heard the shot again, echoing through the torn woods. I clutched Brandon's arm and looked up at him appealingly.

He glanced down at me, saw what he saw, and said, "Pa, I don't think she can bear any more."

Pa scowled. "Sit down," he told me.

I turned to go to the couch behind me, still holding Brandon's arm.

That's all I remember. I don't think I hit the floor, because both Joel and Brandon saw what was about to happen and caught me first.

Brandon picked me up. Somebody, likely Joel, shoved something under my nose and I came to.

"She's been in a bad way since we found her, Pa." I heard this from a distance, as if it was coming through a tunnel, from Joel. "She sat there alone with him for some hours. She was in shock when we found her. I think she still is. She needs something."

"Go in my surgery," I heard Pa say, "and get some—" And then his voice was lost in the tunnel and I was carried upstairs, likely by Brandon. My dress and shoes were taken off and I was put to bed.

I opened my eyes once to see Joel leaning over me with some kind of a powder and water, telling me to take it. I did so. I heard them agree to "take turns through the night."

I woke a lot through the night. I woke crying, sometimes screaming, "Please, David, please—give him what he wants. He's got a gun."

Or I'd say, "The wind, David, the wind is taking you away."

Or, "No more mouth, David. I won't give you any more mouth. I promise, you come back to us and I won't give you any more mouth."

Once I clutched Joel's sleeve and begged him, "I promise I'll be good if you come back. You must come back. Josie is waiting for you."

In between these outbursts I tossed and turned, but every time I woke one of them was in the big armchair beside my bed. Just the sight of a figure there comforted me.

When I opened my eyes in the morning, the sky was blue and sun shone in the windows. Joel was sleeping in the armchair. Outside birds sang.

I slipped out of bed, just a bit shaky and aware that I was still wearing only my chemise and petticoat. I reached for my summer robe and went over to him. I touched the side of his face. He opened his eyes and smiled at me.

"You all right?"

"I'm middling well."

He took me on his lap.

"How," I asked, "can God give us a blue sky and sun and singing birds, like it's an ordinary day, when David is dead?"

He shook his head as if to rid it of cobwebs. "I haven't even had my coffee yet," he told me.

I waited.

"Maybe," he said then, "it's David's job up in heaven right now to wind up the handles that start the birds singing and the sun shining and make the sky blue. You wouldn't want him to fail in his duties on his first day there, would you?"

Only Joel would come up with something like that. I buried my face in his chest and he patted my head. "That doesn't make any sense," I said.

"It doesn't? You know that for a fact?"

"No."

"Makes as much sense to me as anything else does these days. Maybe more. Now let's go downstairs. I need my coffee."

CHAPTER TWENTY-THREE

MY BROTHERS' cavalry unit was called back to the army on the twentieth of July. Where they were going off to we did not know. I cried and hugged them both when they left. I had baked sugar cookies and gave each a package for their haversacks as they sat their horses in front of the house.

They promised to write, then rode off to where the rest of their men were bivouacked at the southeast outskirts of town.

The only brothers I had now. I went back into the house.

Pa was going back to his doctoring tomorrow. There would be no men around. I would miss David more than ever. He was a hole inside me.

❦

THE HOUSE was haunted, but the resident ghost was not David after all. It was Josie. She went about silently, scarcely there, gliding from one room to another, doing her chores, the same chores she'd always done.

At one point after the boys and Pa had left, I heard

her ask Mama, "Do you want me to stay? Do I remind you too much of David?"

"Of course I want you to stay," Mama assured her. "If you want to. Do we remind you too much of David?"

"No. This is like my home here, and—"

"And what, child?"

"Nothing." But she'd been about to say something important, then stopped, changed her mind. I knew Josie enough by now to realize that she had a serious matter on her mind. I also knew that she would come out with it when the time was right. And it was not right yet.

"I can go home to my own mother if you want me to," she added.

"Nonsense." Mama was firm. "Your mama was going to sell the house here and stay with her sister, wasn't she?"

Josie lowered her eyes. "Yes, when David and I married. But now she's keeping it for me, for when I want it."

"Do you want it, Josie?" Mama asked carefully.

More lowering of the eyes. "Not just yet. I'm not ready to be alone yet."

Mama hugged her. "Neither are we, are we, Tacy?"

I said no, we weren't.

❧

MARY AND BASIL Biggs sent Marvelous back to live with us. They had to repair their house and had lost a lot of money in damage of possessions they'd owned, so Mary was living with one of the church women. And Basil with

Sam Weaver, who'd given him the contract to carry bodies from the field to the cemetery.

So it was that Marvelous came again to be with us.

Mama gave her the room Josie had used, for Josie now had David's chamber.

The whole house was askew. Or was it my brain? I still was not sure. All I was sure of was that I would never be right again.

In early September I went back to school. Mama insisted upon it although I saw no sense in French or elocution or dancing classes, and did not care about the proper pitch in which to sing "The Star-Spangled Banner" or that *sugar cain* was supposed to be *sugar cane,* and when it is absolutely unforgivable not to curtsy.

As for geography, in times before we'd been studying the states, which were states and which were still territories. Now nobody knew what states still belonged to us. I'd forgotten, and did not care to remember, what territories were slave or free. Nobody wanted to know.

As for manners, must one curtsy when a man takes his leave after shooting one's brother?

Was it indelicate to raise your skirt in front of your brother to rip off pieces of your petticoat to stanch his blood when he was bleeding to death?

And what if your best friend is a Negro and she is living with you and you start to have doubts about the friendship because you realize of a sudden that the Negroes are the reason for the war. All along it never bothered you that she was a Negro.

But of a sudden it did. Around the tenth of August it did. When they sent the telegram that brought the news that your pa had been killed.

Your *pa!* Who was supposed to be around forever! A doctor! The person who fixed other people when they got hurt or sick. Which was why they'd sent him somewhere in Virginia along with the Union cavalry. The Union cavalry, which meant the Second Pennsylvania with them, Brandon and Joel's unit, to ferret out the Confederates in the area of Brandy Station for some insane army reason.

Joel had told me that most of the army's reasoning was insane, that there had been nothing but insanity behind Lee's reasoning for Pickett's Charge.

So there on the tenth of August, Josie and I had Mama on the floor in the hallway, having fainted with the telegram in her hand that told her Pa had been killed. And Josie and I were kneeling over her. All because the Union army had to go south of the Rappahannock with the cavalry to mark the end of the Gettysburg Campaign.

They had to mark its end?

They hadn't had enough?

No. A whole week the Yankees had to run after them, the cavalry with swords flashing, to have what they called "action," which was their fancy word for killing.

And Pa had to go along. We found out later that it was his own idea. That he'd volunteered to go. Oh, this family is wonderful in the art of volunteering. Josie and I figured out that he went along to be near Brandon and Joel because he'd lost David and he was blaming himself for that. Oh, this family is wonderful in the art of guilt, too.

So there was Pa, all set up with other doctors in a tent hospital. But unlike the other doctors, he volunteered to run out of the tent when the fighting died down to help bring the wounded in.

Because he'd heard one of the wounded was Brandon.

But the thing is, the battle was not yet completely over. A Rebel sniper fired at Pa from somewhere in the bushes. And everyone, from both North and South, knows you don't shoot at doctors. Because if that same sniper were wounded and lying half dead on the ground, or even half alive, Pa would have gone to his aid and fixed him up, proper-like. Everybody knows that.

But this Rebel sniper shot Pa dead, right there on the field. And somebody else brought Brandon in.

And here is where what David once said comes into it.

"God has a sense of humor," David once told me.

I must agree with him.

Brandon was slashed in the leg by a Rebel cavalry officer. His cavalry days were over.

We were advised of that by another telegram, which arrived on the eleventh of August. The United States Army, or whichever entity was responsible for sending such matter through the mails, was considerate enough not to let the two telegrams arrive on the same day.

So you see why, when I went back to the Young Ladies' Seminary in September, I did not give an owl's hoot
whether it is spelled *sugar cain* or *sugar cane*. As a matter
of fact, I think I shall spell it *sugar cain* for the rest of
my life.

CHAPTER TWENTY-FOUR

GOD'S SENSE OF humor has gone beyond all perception of bounds. And if I am to be consigned to hell for this, then so be it.

When we buried Pa, he and Mama were married twenty-seven years to the day. In 1836, back in Richmond, Virginia.

I wondered, standing there in the cemetery while the reverend read the prayer about the valley of death, if Mama minded that this was her wedding anniversary.

She was standing between Joel and Brandon, leaning on Joel, because Brandon was leaning on his sword. He was still in his uniform and he could scarce hold himself up.

Josie stood a bit apart with Marvelous and her mother and daddy.

Around us were near a hundred people who'd known Pa. Someone was playing a violin. Pa was being buried right next to David. And although it was the middle of a bright August afternoon, many of the mourners held lighted candles.

I looked up at Brandon. I touched the sleeve of his

short cavalryman's jacket that tucked into his black pistol belt. "Brandon," I said softly.

He looked down at me and smiled.

"Today is Mama and Pa's wedding anniversary," I whispered.

He nodded. He knew. But he lifted a hand and put his forefinger across my lips and shook his head no.

I saw Brandon's wound. I saw Joel dress it. Brandon had claimed that it was "just a scratch." "I don't know why they made such a fuss about it," he said. "I don't know why they mustered me out."

"It cut into your muscle," Joel told him, "that's why. You're lucky it didn't cut into the bone."

I saw where it had been stitched up, saw the ugly red mass and covered my mouth and said "Oh" before my brothers even realized I was in Joel's room. He was kneeling at Brandon's feet. Brandon was on the bed, his pant leg shoved all the way above his knee. Both were startled and looked up.

Joel scowled. "Now," he said sternly, "you just turn yourself around and get out of here, miss."

When Joel was displeased with me he called me "miss."

"I just wanted to make sure Brandon is all right."

"He's going to be home from now on. You have plenty of time to make sure. Go." The tone was as severe as I'd ever heard from Joel, who'd always spoiled me.

I turned, crying at the rebuke, and fled.

Later he came to me and kissed me. "I'm sorry I scolded," he said. "It's difficult for all of us with Pa gone

and Brandon temporarily incapacitated. The family struc-
ture is broken. We're all fumbling around, trying to put it
together again."

Joel had to report back within a week, but he and
Brandon had long confabs, some with Mama, before he
left. I begged not to go back to school, but Mama was
adamant and my brothers laid down the law.

"They won't hear of your staying home," Mama said.

They? We were sitting around the parlor on a pleasant
August evening with the windows open and the lace cur-
tains fluttering, for there was something unusual happening. An August breeze that hinted of fall. Fall, with all the
anguished summer memories to be forgotten.

They? My brothers were sipping coffee. Brandon had
already had a visit from Dr. Henry Baugher, president of
the Pennsylvania College, asking him to come back to his
old teaching position as soon as he was able.

They? I looked at the faces, one at a time, of my mama
and then Joel and Brandon.

"What do you mean *they,* Mama?" I asked. "You know
I love Brandon and Joel, but since when are they making
the decisions?"

I saw Brandon lower his head and try to hide a smile.
Joel didn't try to hide it. He leaned back in the chair instead and lit a cheroot.

"Well, darling," Mama said in her most reasonable
voice, "you know how it is out there in the world. Women
are always better off when men run things. In matters of
money and commerce and all decisions that have to do

with lawyers and legal matters, why, it's always so much better when men run things. Women are treated with hostile attitudes when they try to take over the place of men. Your father knew this, and so he set things up in his will. That when he died, your older brothers were to be in charge of your welfare."

I nodded slowly.

"When I grow up," I said, "the world is going to be a different place. Women are going to be allowed to do things."

"You mean," Joel asked, "that you don't like the idea of us looking after you?"

"I thought you loved us," from Brandon. He looked at his brother. "Fickle," he said. "See that? Didn't I tell you all women are fickle?"

Joel nodded. "You were right. But then, you usually are when it comes to women. Remember that girl back in—"

"Never mind." Brandon stopped him short.

Tears came into my eyes. I'd hurt their feelings. Joel was going away to fight and Brandon was wounded. I ran first to Joel, threw myself into his lap, and hugged him. "I'd rather have nobody else," I told him. "And you just take care of yourself."

I held him tight, then ran to Brandon, sat on the arm of his chair, and flung my arms around his neck. "You won't be sorry," I said.

"I know that, or I would have turned down the job."

He tweaked my nose. "Though something tells me I'll have a lot of work to do."

He smiled again and it came to me. Today, this evening in this parlor, was the first time he'd smiled since he'd come home wounded. Something told me that I had a lot of work to do, too.

CHAPTER TWENTY-FIVE

IT WAS MAMA who noticed the chilling distance that had developed between me and Marvelous. And she went and told Brandon that something was not right between us.

Soon after Joel left, Brandon spoke to me about it.

He'd been staying quiet a lot, healing his leg and studying, getting his work ready for the classes he was going to teach when he went back to the college. Literature, history, and philosophy.

Mama had been busying herself making me new dresses for when I returned to school. There was a shortage of good fabric, but her sister in Philadelphia had sent some.

She was even sewing up some frocks for Marvelous, who was being tutored privately by a Quaker woman, along with two other negro girls in Gettysburg.

"Have you and Marvelous had a fight?" Mama asked me one day when she was pinning up the hem of one of my dresses.

"No, Mama."

"You don't talk so much anymore. And you used to help her with her reading."

I shrugged. "She doesn't want me to," I lied. "She wants to see if she can do it herself. She feels uncomfortable because she doesn't read as well as I do."

Mama gave me a cautious look but said nothing. My mama is not stupid. She knew I was lying.

That evening when Marvelous had gone over to the church to have supper with her mother, as usual, Mama went with her, which was not usual, and it was only me and Brandon and Josie at the table.

After supper Mama and I, Brandon, and Josie would always retire to the parlor to catch up on things. This evening Josie excused herself and I was left with my brother.

He wasted no time. "Would you get me that ottoman for my leg, honey? I like to prop it up."

I fetched it and set it before him. As I did, he held my wrist, pulled me down, and set me on the ottoman. "We have to talk," he said.

"What did I do?"

He smiled. "Don't look so guilty. I don't know if you did anything. Ma is concerned. She says you and Marvelous aren't getting on anymore. Is this true?"

"Oh, that."

"Then it is true. Is there a problem?"

Tears came into my eyes. "I don't know, Brandon. If there is, I don't know if I can even talk about it."

"That bad, huh?"

Now the tears started down my face. I looked at him appealingly. "It's terrible, Brandon, it's just terrible!"

He took out a handkerchief and wiped my face. "Why don't you just try telling me. Maybe it isn't so terrible after all."

"Do you promise not to tell Mama? Or anybody?"

He hesitated a moment, then nodded yes.

I sniffed then, and told him. "I love Marvelous. Always have. We've always been best friends. Until—" I had to stop to stifle a sob and begin again. "Until the day the telegram came that told us Pa was killed." I stopped and looked at him.

He did not understand. He raised his eyebrows and waited.

"And then the next day the one came about you being wounded. Mama went crazy. You don't know what she was like, Brandon. You don't know what it was like for me and Josie."

He was eyeing me carefully, nodding his head slowly.

"What," he asked, "has all this to do with Marvelous?"

I lowered my head, aware that he was watching me studiously, aware also that he already knew what it had to do with Marvelous but waiting to hear it from me.

I did not answer. I could not answer.

"Tell me, Tacy," he said.

"You already know," I accused.

"I want to hear you say the words."

"Why?"

"Because if you can think them, you can say them. And if you say them, you will realize how stupid they sound. So say them. Now. To me."

"I started to realize then," I choked, half crying, "that Pa was killed and, and you, you were wounded, because of the war. And—" I hiccupped. "I can't, can't, Brandon . . ."

"Say the words, Tacy."

". . . and the war happened to free the Negroes. And so I didn't like her anymore. Because it was on account of her and her kind. So there, I've said it, damn you!"

I burst into full-fledged crying then and started to get up, but he grabbed my arm and wouldn't let me. He leaned forward in the chair, put his arms around me, and held me fast.

I leaned against him, bawling. He patted my back, my hair. He shushed me.

"Am I bad?" I asked.

"No, you're just confused. We all are. We're all questioning things we hold dear and those we love. We have to, because everything we know is on the line and we're being tested, and when we come through, and we will, we'll all be stronger. And we'll find the things we hold dear and those we love will still be there, better than always."

"I'm so glad you're here, Brandon, I really am."

"So am I."

"You're not going to punish me for saying 'damn you'?"

"Next time," he said, "I promise."

I drew back to look at him. "I don't really dislike Marvelous or blame her for anything. I was more afraid of myself because I was thinking that way."

"Then you make it up to Marvelous," he said. "Promise me."

"How?"

"You'll think of a way. Just promise me."

So I did.

EPILOGUE

Iᴺ ʟᴀᴛᴇ ᴀᴜɢᴜꜱᴛ Brandon received a circular from the lawyer who had handled Pa's will, Mr. David Mc-Conaughy.

I usually took in the mail, and so I stood next to Brandon while he read it.

"Mr. McConaughy," he told me, "is also the president of the Board of Evergreen Cemetery."

What McConaughy and a man named David Wills wanted was land laid aside in Gettysburg for a national cemetery for the men killed in the battle.

A note that came, too, said that the circular was sent only to "the town's most prominent citizens." McConaughy wanted a Memorial Association to oversee the operation. And he wanted Brandon to be on it.

Between his teaching and his meetings for the new cemetery, Brandon was very busy. And several of the meetings were held at our house.

The meeting at which Mr. Wills came up with the idea to invite President Lincoln took place there. I remember that Mr. Wills was eating my chocolate cake when he said this.

The date was set for November 19, 1863.

BECAUSE HE WAS on the Memorial Association, my brother Brandon was at the train station in Gettysburg the day President Abraham Lincoln came to our town at six in the evening.

He met the president, shook his hand, and was introduced as a war hero.

Mama was on one of the committees to plan the food to feed the thousands of people who came. Every house had opened its doors to supply sandwiches and coffee and cake, and Josie and Marvelous and I were stationed at our house to do so.

The weather was mild for a November day. Our house was dressed up in American flags. Cassie wore a red, white, and blue kerchief around her neck.

But first we had to go to hear the president's speech, all of us.

I did not hear it, though I was there, right next to Josie.

I did not hear, at ten a.m. the next day, the words that were to become so famous, the words people would never forget. Because right after "Four score and seven years ago," Josie whispered to me the words I would never forget.

"Tacy," she said, "I have to tell you. I'm pregnant. I'm going to have David's baby."

AND SO IT was that we would, henceforth, have a little bit of David with us always.

Mama was happy, Brandon was happy, and I was happy. And Josie continued to live with us, though Mama refused to have her work for us anymore and had to hire someone else instead.

She hired a woman named Nancy Buckrin, who had been a nurse during the war and gone everywhere from working for Dorothea Dix in Washington, to the fields of Antietam, to Gettysburg. She was thirty-five years old and after Gettysburg had seen enough, she told Brandon, who interviewed and hired her. And she did not wish either to marry or to go home to New York State, but she wanted the comfort of being with a family.

There are so many things to say that I could go on forever, but I will say only that the war went on for two more years. That Brandon and Emily Sedgwick did not wed, for she'd never come back from that trip to Philadelphia, never inquired after him when he was wounded. But now he is seeing Isabella McKay, only daughter of one of the professors at the college.

Brandon has proved to be very good to me, very kind. As I said, we never argue. When I do something not to his liking he can be quietly stern, but never as much as when I sass Mama. He will simply not abide that for any reason.

I love him so, that I go out of my way not to offend him. We are good friends.

As for Marvelous, the only way I can put it is that she is the sister I never had.

There are things that should be put down here.

The young officer Lieutenant Stover, who gave me his sword to keep that day so long ago, never came back for it, so I suppose he was killed. I have the sword still. Brandon said I should keep it.

About Culp's Hill. The Culps, for whom the hill was named, had two sons, Wesley and William. Before the war, Wesley left Gettysburg and went south, where he married a Southern girl and lived in Virginia. When the war came he enlisted in the Second Virginia. He died in the fight on Culp's Hill. His brother William enlisted in the Eighty-seventh Pennsylvania.

❧

IN AUGUST we learned that Johnston Hastings Skelly, who was engaged to wed Jennie Wade, and who was with the Eighty-seventh Pennsylvania Volunteers, had been shot at Winchester, Virginia, on the fifteenth of June, two weeks before the battle of Gettysburg. Jennie Wade had never received word of it. Skelly died on the twelfth of July and he did not know that Jennie was already dead.

Joel came home to us unscarred from the war, and went back to medical school.

Josie's baby was a boy. She named him David.

People are coming to our town in droves to go to the battlefields for specimens. Everyone wants a relic of

Gettysburg. On November 16, the *Compiler* ran an article that said, "The trunks of two trees have been sent from the battlefield of Gettysburg (Culp's Hill) for the Pennsylvania and Massachusetts historical societies. One of them has two hundred and fifty bullet holes in the space of twenty-one feet, and the other one hundred and ten in the same space. These specimens attest to the fierceness of the fighting."

But in our hearts, here in the Stryker house, we have other specimens that attest to the fierceness of the fighting. As has everyone in Gettysburg.

And then there is this:

Those trees on Culp's Hill that waved in the wind that night when I sat holding my brother David's head in my lap when he died, all those beautiful, wounded trees eventually died of lead poisoning. But they still wave their branches in my heart.

AUTHOR'S NOTE

I WAS HESITANT, at first, to write yet another novel about Gettysburg. So many have been written, so many excellent ones. Did I dare even approach the subject with so much competition out there?

Then, simply because I could not restrain myself, I started to research the subject anyway. And I found things that I had never read about, matters never touched on in any novel I had read about Gettysburg, or, if touched on, just mentioned in passing. These were things that were never made an important part of any story, never integrated into any story; yet they jumped out and hit me in the face.

In particular, I am writing about the presence of between two hundred and four hundred free American black people living and working in the town.

And so I knew that if I made them a part of the story, at the very least, I could do my book and it would be different.

For instance, I intended to focus not on the battle but on my one family in town, the Strykers, fictional people trying to make it through this difficult (to put it mildly) period, as did all the real families in town at the time.

When I was a columnist on the *Trentonian,* the Pulitzer Prize–winning newspaper in Trenton, New Jersey, my editor F. Gilman Spencer (who won the Pulitzer Prize), always told me, when a major story or event or riot broke out in town (as often happened), "Go out in the streets, Ann, and talk to the everyday people and get their reactions, their feelings."

So that was my "beat." The everyday people. And still, in my novels now, I make it my beat, as I did in this one. I was not there in the middle of Pickett's Charge, or on Culp's Hill (until after the battle, anyway) or on Little Roundtop.

I was with Tacy Stryker in the Stryker House. I was with her when she went to visit Jennie Wade, her longtime friend, and argued with her. I was with her when she ran off in the night to find her friend Marvelous and bring her home, when she and the other girls ran off to the Lutheran Theological Seminary, to the top floor, to look out with binoculars at the world around them.

I was with her when she visited Marvelous and her mother in Christ Lutheran Church, and when she shivered, frightened, in the cellar of her home with the others, while shells exploded all around them.

There are no particular acts of bravery in the book for Tacy to accomplish. Through most of it she is scared, confused, uncertain, angry, and, in general, making the wrong choices, according to her brother David. She asks many questions but gets no final answers.

But she does come through, and that, in the end,

seems to be enough for the moment, when she thought she never would come through, and coming through seems to be a gift for them all.

Still, she has questions. "How can God give us a blue sky and sun and singing birds, like it's an ordinary day, when David is dead?" she asks of her brother Joel.

His answer? He is older, wiser, an officer in the cavalry. He just shakes his head and says, "I haven't even had my coffee yet."

But she also has come to some conclusions: "When I grow up, things are going to be different. Women are going to be allowed to do things." And, as far as her older brother Brandon is concerned, he who is going to look after her and has said, "Something tells me I have a lot of work to do," she thinks:

"Today, is the first time I'd seen him smile in a long time. Something tells me I have a lot of work to do, too."

So as I say, Tacy Stryker has made no great strides in my book to shake up the world, or even the town of Gettysburg. She has not played the part of a spy for the Yankees, run any secret messages, saved the day for General John Buford (as a matter of fact, Buford personally kicked her and her friends out of the Lutheran Theological Seminary).

Of course, she held her brother David until he died on Culp's Hill, when others might have left, where they were burying bodies after the battle was over and he took his stand in guarding the dead. She waited alone in the dark for someone, anyone, to come.

No, she would not leave him there. He was, after all, her brother David, who had been so mean to her after her pa went to war as a surgeon and left him in charge.

So mean. He'd made her cry so many times. How could she leave him here now, alone and dead?

Some would. But not Tacy. So she waited in the dark with his head in her lap, for someone to come.

❦

THE STRYKER FAMILY in my book is fictional. But many of the other characters are true to life as I have found them in research.

Jennie Wade, of course, is not only true to life, but famous.

She was the only civilian to have been killed in the battle of Gettysburg. She and her mother were in the house of her older sister, Mrs. John McClellan, on Baltimore Street, helping her sister with a six-day-old baby. Jennie was kneading bread dough on that Friday morning of the battle when a Rebel sniper's bullet came smashing through the door. It hit Jennie and she slumped to the floor, dead.

In my book I have Jennie Wade in a fictionalized past romance with David Stryker and a friendship with Tacy.

To this day she is a heroine in Gettysburg, Pennsylvania.

General John Buford, of course, is real, as was the unfortunate General John Reynolds, who was killed almost instantly at Gettysburg.

Marvelous is a character of my own creation. Although the man I picked for her father, Basil Biggs, actually lived. He was described in *A Strange and Blighted Land,* one research book I used, as "colored, of Gettysburg, was given the contract for disinterring the bodies on the field. He had a crew of eight or ten negroes in his employ."

Mr. Cameron, as well as Nancy Burns's old grandfather, in his seventies, who went off to fight, and even the horses who ran down the street and through the hallway of the house three doors from Tacy's, I got from research.

I got all the background for my story from research, of course. The rest, the interaction between the characters, I made up. I tried to keep as close as I could to the schedule of the battle going on as I led my characters through their paces; that is, when the shelling started and stopped, when the Rebs were prominent in town, ruling the place and when they were losing and just sneaking about. The provost marshall did issue an order prohibiting the exhuming of bodies. My research shows two conflicting dates for this. *A Strange and Blighted Land* cites August tenth, and *Uncertainty and Dread,* another book I used for research, says, "The business [of exhuming the bodies] was brisk until the heat of the summer became so severe that the Provost Marshall halted the exhuming of graves on the field until the cool of October."

I made my own decision as to the date for the provost marshal's order, for the sake of story.

I do believe that the presence of two hundred to four hundred free black Americans living in Gettysburg at the time of the battle needed to be addressed in some fashion in my book, since it has not, to my knowledge, been in any work of fiction yet published.

Some of those free black Americans were captured when the Rebels came into town and taken into slavery, as Mary told the Strykers when she and Marvelous escaped and fled to the Stryker house. I tried to deal with the possibility of Marvelous being taken when the Confederates forced themselves into the Stryker house and Tacy and Marvelous had to feed them breakfast. It was then that my fictional Private Joel Walker and Private John Calhoun of the Rebel army tell Tacy that because Marvelous is black she is "up for grabs," saying, "We can take this darkie girl here [with us if we want to]."

Now Tacy gets the chance to finally stand up and speak for what she believes in. She speaks out for her friend Marvelous, though she does not know what to say. If she had her brother David's Colt .45, she thinks, she would kill them, never mind that she does not know how to use it. She would learn how to use it. Instead, she uses her words, all she has.

She begs Lieutenant Gregory Lewis Marshall, their

commanding officer, for her friend's freedom, begs him to allow her friend to stay in Gettysburg, free as she is now, and not take her south to be a slave. She uses the only words she has. "She is a good person. And she is my friend."

Fortunately, the lieutenant considers himself insignificant in the scheme of things. Nobody ever asks his opinion about important matters, he tells Tacy. He is never allowed to make decisions. And he himself has lost many friends in this war. But here and now he is being asked to make an important decision and so, by the gods, he will make one.

Marvelous can stay.

Tacy has accomplished something important here, then. No, she has not saved the town. She cannot save her brother David in the end, or her father. Life does to her and all of them what it will. And she still has questions that she needs answered when the book ends. As do we all.

Unfortunately, I cannot answer them all for my readers, but hopefully I have given you all a good read and something to think about.

BIBLIOGRAPHY

Adams, George Worthington. *Doctors in Blue.* Dayton, Ohio: Press of Morningside, 1985.

Alleman, Mrs. Tillie Pierce. *At Gettysburg, or What a Girl Saw and Heard and Saw of the Battle.* New York: W. Lake Borland, 1889.

Bennett, Gerald R. *Uncertainty and Dread: The Ordeal Endured by the Citizens of Gettysburg.* Camp Hill, Pa.: Plank's Suburban Press, 1997.

Burke, Davis. *The Civil War: Strange and Fascinating Facts.* New York: Fairfax Press, 1982.

Coco, Gregory A. *A Strange and Blighted Land: Gettysburg, The Aftermath of a Battle.* Gettysburg, Pa.: Thomas Publications, 1995.

Conklin, E. F. *Women at Gettysburg, 1863.* Gettysburg, Pa.: Thomas Publications, 1993.

Faust, Patricia L., editor. *Historical Times Illustrated Encyclopedia of the Civil War.* New York: Harper and Row Publishers, 1986.

Varhola, Michael J. *Everyday Life During the Civil War: A Guide for Writers, Students and Historians.* Cincinnati, Ohio: Writer's Digest Books, 1999.

Williams, William G. *Days of Darkness: Gettysburg Civilians.* New York: Berkley Books, 1990.